HERBS AND HOMICIDE

A SMALL TOWN COZY MYSTERY

CARLY WINTER

Edited by
DIVAS AT WORK EDITING

Cover by
COVEREDBYMELINDA.COM

WESTWARD PUBLISHING / CARLY FALL, LLC

HERBS AND HOMICIDE

From Hollywood, California, to Heywood, Arizona, trouble follows her...

After her husband's brutal killing and her fall from the Hollywood elite, the disgraced Samantha Rathbone moves to Heywood hoping to forget her past and live a quiet life of anonymity as Sam Jones.

When she takes a job at the local herbal shop, Sage Advice, and the owner is found murdered, Sam is pushed back into the unwanted spotlight when she becomes the number one suspect. As she wades through ugly family drama, the questionable business practices of others, and the lies embroiled in a small town, she searches for the true killer, hoping to save herself.

Will Samantha be able to find the murderer before she's put away for a crime she didn't commit?

CHAPTER 1

I SLAMMED ON THE BRAKES, closed my eyes, and gripped the steering wheel so tightly, I briefly worried it might snap in my hands. For a few seconds, I thought about dying, my life flashing before my eyes. My horrible childhood. My rise to fame and fortune. The crash and burn when it was all taken away from me. I'd come darn close to death once, and it seemed it may be knocking on my door again. And this time, I still wasn't ready.

I waited for the impact from the front, but thankfully, it never came. Instead, my vehicle stopped with the sound of crunching metal from the passenger's side. As I opened my eyes, I released my grip on the steering wheel, my hands aching. I'd overcorrected and landed in the trees on the side of the road. Across the two-lane highway stood the deer I'd almost hit.

As our gazes met, I sighed in relief. Such a beautiful animal. One that could've easily killed me if it had come through the windshield after impact.

I opened my door and it sprinted away into the forest. Groaning, I stood. Every muscle in my back and shoulders tensed. I walked around the front of my white BMW to study the damage, thankful the cool breeze calmed my raging hot flash. Menopause was the worst.

Impact had taken place at the front wheel panel and the door. The tire had crushed inward at a strange angle, and my door no longer followed the lines of the car, the bottom protruding outward. Car meets tree; tree wins.

With a sigh, I pulled out my phone. No service, either. The day was going splendidly. I took some deep breaths and tried to calm my racing heart.

It hadn't started out this way. I'd risen early and driven to Sedona, Arizona, to pick up some fresh herbs for the herbal apothecary I worked at in Heywood. The trip had provided me with breathtaking views of the red rocks Sedona had to offer, gorgeous sights of the forest, and a lot of time to relax and think about my life, something I didn't like to do. I was busy rebuilding from a past that had brought me anger, bitterness, and profound sadness.

I leaned against the driver's side. Hopefully, someone would come around. Heywood was about fifteen miles up the road and the residents I'd met were very nice people. Hopefully someone I knew would stop to give me a ride. Until then, I'd soak up the fresh air and the sounds of the forest surrounding me.

Birds. The wind whispering through the large firs. A squirrel crossing the road. Nature at its best.

Ten minutes later, a pickup truck pulled up behind my car. A huge man standing over six feet exited, clad in coveralls and a thick gray beard. With his bright smile and being in his seventies, he reminded me of Santa.

But bad things always happened when a man approached a woman in the middle of the forest. Dozens of slasher movies had proved that.

"What happened?" he asked as he approached.

"I almost had a run-in with a deer."

"Well, at least it wasn't a Sasquatch encounter." Was he serious? He shook his head and placed his hands on his hips as he studied the damage, but his face remained somber, which made me wonder. "You okay?"

"Yes. Thank you."

He walked around to the front of the car, giving me a wide berth, which made me feel slightly safer. "You're not going anywhere," he said, assessing the damage.

"I know."

"Did you call someone?"

"No." I held up my phone. "No service out here."

"Figures. No one has service in these parts, no matter who their carrier is. Where you headed?" he asked, running a hand over his beard.

"Heywood. I live there."

"I've got a farm on the other side of Heywood, so I can give you a lift if you like."

Pursing my lips, I'd been hoping it was just my phone provider that didn't cover the area and he'd be able to make a call for me. Getting into a stranger's car wasn't something I was too keen on doing.

"I'm not going to bite," he said, holding both hands up in front of him. "I'm one of the good guys."

And Ted Bundy had probably claimed the same thing.

Quickly weighing my options, I realized I didn't like either. I could walk, or I could accept his offer.

"My name's Charlie Tupper," he said, stretching out his hand. "I've lived in the area my whole life. My family has been farming the same piece of land for four generations."

With a sigh, I took his calloused palm. I'd have to trust him. "Sam Jones," I said. "Thank you for helping me."

"Sure. Come on, Ms. Jones. Let's get you home."

I grabbed my package of herbs from the backseat of my car and crawled into the cab of Charlie's truck. I was met by a Golden Retriever in the back seat who promptly said hello by licking my face.

"That's Daisy," Charlie said. "If she's anything, it's over-friendly, so I apologize in advance."

While Daisy's tail thumped against the seat, she tasted my cheek once again and I ran my hand over her soft head. I felt a little better having accepted the ride from Charlie. No rapist or killer would own a dog like her.

"Anyone ever tell you that you look like that

actress? What's her name… Andi McDowell?" He pulled out on the highway.

I smiled and kept my gaze focused on the road ahead. "Yes, I've heard that before." Many times, in fact. Once, I was told that I looked just like the actress, except I wasn't as pretty. But that had been in my former life, the one I was trying to forget.

"So, where are you from? You didn't grow up around these parts, or I'd know of you."

"Los Angeles. I moved to Heywood about three months ago."

"Huh. Los Angeles to Heywood is a pretty big jump. What happened? Did Mickey Mouse chase you out of town?"

I chuckled, but he had no idea how close he was to the truth.

"How do you like the little gem in the forest?" Charlie asked.

Pausing a moment, I considered my answer. I was still raw from my previous life burning to the ground both figuratively and literally, but every day I seemed to heal just a bit more. I appreciated my job and the knowledge I was gaining, and I did love Heywood—a little town situated on the banks of a river nestled in the middle of the forest. "I really like it," I said, meaning every word. "It's beautiful."

He spoke of a few people in town, asking if I knew them. A couple, I'd met. Most, I hadn't. "What about Bonnie?" he asked. "She runs Sage Advice."

"She's my boss," I replied, grinning while I pet Daisy again. "I live in the apartment upstairs from her store."

Charlie laughed and tapped his hand against the steering wheel, obviously thrilled we knew someone in common. "Ah… Bonnie and I have some history. She's a good woman. Do you like goats?"

From Bonnie to goats. The change in conversation threw me off a bit. "I'm… I'm not really sure." Had I ever met one? I couldn't recall. They weren't a common sight in Hollywood, but I thought of my travels abroad and still came up empty.

As I listened to his tales of baby goats and building a petting zoo on his farm for his grandkids, I found myself enjoying his company and the simplicity of his life as he described it—a direct contradiction to the existence I'd left three months ago. Back then, I'd been lectured about being a fifty-four-year-old woman, my weight, whether or not I needed more Botox, and why in the world did I have gray hair?

But that was Hollywood. I much preferred the minimalism of Heywood.

"We've got miniature cows as well," Charlie continued. "Cutest dang things I've ever seen. You should come out sometime and see them and the baby chickens. Little balls of yellow fluff running around. The grandkids love them."

By the time he dropped me off in front of Sage Advice, we'd exchanged phone numbers, and he made me promise I'd be out to see his farm soon.

I smiled as I entered the store.

"Sam!" Bonnie said, rounding the counter. "I've been worried sick! Where have you been?"

She embraced me, and I closed my eyes for a second, appreciating the warmth and concern. "I almost hit a deer. Instead, I ended up in the ditch. Charlie Tupper stopped to help me."

"Oh, he's a good man," she said, holding me at arm's length and studying me from head to toe. "You don't look injured. Are you?"

I shook my head. "I'm fine. My car isn't, though. I need to call a tow truck."

"Go ahead and do what you need to do," she

replied, taking the bag of herbs from me. "I'll take these in back."

"Do you mind if I go upstairs?" I asked. My neck had started to ache and a cool cloth, along with some ibuprofen, had become mandatory.

"Of course not, dear. Take your time. I've got nowhere to be but here." As she smiled, her face wrinkled up like a Shar-Pei puppy's, but her eyes twinkled with youth and health. In her seventies, she was the most vibrant person I'd ever met.

I followed her through the back room, then headed up the stairs to my apartment. When I'd first arrived in Heywood three months ago, I'd had very little money, no job, and nowhere to live. Bonnie had been my savior, providing me with all of the above.

As I made some turmeric and vanilla tea in the small kitchen, I waited on hold for my insurance agent. When I explained the accident and gave her the mile marker where the car could be found, she promised to take care of it and have the car towed to the garage in Heywood, Tinkering on Trucks. After they examined it, she'd be back in touch.

I sat for a few moments with a cool cloth on my head. Good thing Heywood was small enough that I could walk from one end to the other. Honestly, I almost hoped they totaled the BMW. It was the last reminder of my former life, and I liked the idea of driving one of those big Ford F150s, preferably in cherry red. Or, if they did total it, I could pocket the money since I really didn't need a vehicle to get around in Heywood.

Voices filtered up the stairs, which wasn't an odd occurrence. Living above the store, I always heard people talking during business hours. However, this wasn't a normal conversation. No. Someone was very, very angry.

I stood and hurried out of my apartment, taking the stairs two at a time. Rushing through the back room, I found Bonnie behind the counter, smiling, while Doctor Garrett Butte yelled at her.

"You can't just prescribe any potion you come up with to my patients!" he screamed, his face so red, if he dropped dead of a heart attack, I wouldn't be surprised. Considering he was the same age as Bonnie, it wasn't a far-fetched idea.

"I don't prescribe anything," Bonnie said. "What I do is suggest what herbs may help with someone's malady and advise they talk to their doctor about using them."

"Herbs aren't medicine!" he yelled. "They're

plants! What you do here is nothing short of witchcraft!"

Bonnie rolled her eyes. "Garrett, don't be silly. I've told you this a dozen times. Herbs have been used for centuries around the world by almost every culture to promote health and healing. Not all good things come in a prescription bottle."

"I don't want you messing with my patients!" he said, pointing his finger at her face.

"Is this about Debra?" Bonnie asked, crossing her arms over her chest.

His bluster faded for a brief moment.

"She hasn't had any issues with her G.E.R.D., has she?"

Garrett remained silent.

"Here's the deal, doc," Bonnie continued. "You've had her on four different medications over the past six months, most of which did nothing, or only helped for a short while. She came to me asking for help. I gave her some ginger and chamomile but told her to go see you before taking it. I'm sorry she didn't follow my advice."

His face paled into a somewhat normal color for a white man in his seventies.

"But isn't the fact that she's feeling better the result we all wanted?" Bonnie asked.

Left speechless, Garrett shook his head and stormed out of the store.

"What was that all about?" I asked.

Bonnie sighed as she stared at the door. "There will always be a war between herbal medicine and pharmaceutical medicine, Sam. He's upset I was able to treat Debra so easily. Gone are her monthly visits to his office, and all the drugs he's prescribing. Some doctors even get kickbacks for drugs they give their patients, so he may have lost money there, as well. For him, it's not about curing, but managing enough so the patient needs to keep coming back." She shook her head and shrugged. "More office visits, more drugs."

"You think he'd just be happy his patient is feeling better."

"You'd think," she said. "But Garrett has been angry at me for years because my "silly" plants always seem to outperform his pills. This isn't the first time he's been in here screaming at me, and I assure you, it won't be the last. If that man put a knife in my back tomorrow, I wouldn't be surprised."

CHAPTER 2

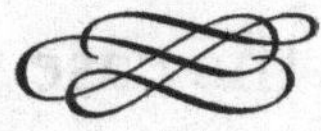

WHEN I'D ARRIVED in Heywood three months ago, one of the first things I had done was walk into Sage Advice. Call it karma, kismet... whatever. There had been two simple reasons: first, I had a passing interest in herbs and their healing abilities. I was a hobbyist. Second, I'd gone from wealthy to almost flat broke in a matter of days, and I desperately needed a job. At that time, I'd told Bonnie I knew enough about herbalism to realize I didn't know much, and she'd hired me on the spot. Who could've guessed that would be the right answer?

The first thing she taught me was the language of an herbalist. We were not doctors. We didn't diagnose, treat, or prescribe. We educated and consulted. We spoke of balance and nurturing our bodies. People needed doctors and should see them for their concerns. Bonnie had shared that many times, her store was the last stop for a frustrated person who just wanted a bit of relief, as had been the case with Debra.

I'd been at the store the day Debra had come in with tears in her eyes. Not only had she been on numerous medications, but Dr. Butte was also talking about scoping her stomach and running other tests, which Debra didn't want to do unless absolutely necessary.

"I can't afford all that, even with insurance," she'd said, wiping the tears tracking down her cheeks. "I'd have to save up for months. I just want to sleep through the night without my stomach feeling like it's on fire."

Bonnie had gone over her diet, told her to cut out the fried foods and sent her on her way with some ginger and chamomile capsules, along with the warning to consult her doctor about taking them. Apparently, Debra hadn't heard that part— or simply chose to ignore it. Dr. Butte seemed truly angry at how easy it had been to help Debra. A change in diet, a couple of soothing plants. Who would have thought?

Not all doctors were bad, but if what Bonnie

had said about Garrett Butte was true, he fell into that category.

The second thing Bonnie had taught me in my short time was that I had a long way to go to educate myself. Some herbs shouldn't be taken with others. Some shouldn't be taken with modern day medication. Bonnie had thick tomes full of recipes and information for me to study and digest, which I did in every free moment. I appreciated the focus needed in order to learn as it kept my thoughts from straying to my past and me wallowing in the hurt and bitterness.

Before opening the store the next morning, I did some yoga in my little living room. Going from a six thousand square foot house to my one-bedroom apartment had been quite the culture shock at first, and had even resulted in me experiencing some claustrophobia. However, the small space had grown on me quickly. Done in pastel greens and blues, I found the apartment soothing and comforting.

After my yoga, I had two cups of coffee, and scanned my laptop for any news about me in my former life. I hadn't found anything in the past month, but I continued to search. Did they think I was alive? Dead? Did anyone in Hollywood really care at this point? And why should *I* bother about their speculations? Because I'd walked away from the fraudulent mess my husband had made and I probably should've stayed to see it fully cleaned up. But, I hadn't—and I'd yet to regret it. If I had someone coming after me, be it law enforcement or a hit man one of my former colleagues had hired, I wanted to be as aware as possible. Had I broken any laws? I didn't think so. I'd done nothing wrong, but had been caught up in my husband's crimes nonetheless.

I grabbed a quick bowl of cereal and almond milk, took my herbs to promote cell regeneration and energy, then headed downstairs. As I strode past Bonnie's apartment, I didn't hear her television on, which was odd. Usually, she'd be watching the morning news. Maybe she'd been up reading late into the night, which also happened frequently.

After I flipped on the lights in the store, I did a quick dusting of the glass display tables containing different soap sets we'd made, and specialty teas and tinctures, each arranged in a way that really focused on the colors and beauty of the product. The shelves on the right-hand wall showcasing glass bottles of dried herbs stretched to the ceiling, requiring me to pull out a small ladder to reach the top. Each bottle was marked with a color-coded label and wording written in a calligraphy flourishing style, all of which was my doing. I'd discovered I had a talent for displaying our goods in such a manner, and our sales increased by twenty percent since I'd arrived. I may not know all the ins and outs of herbs, but I apparently could rock a display like no one's business.

"Good morning, good morning!"

I turned to find Annabelle Granger, another employee, strolling in through the front door. Even though she was about my age, she was a California Valley Girl firmly stuck in the 80s in her attire. She wore her bleached blonde hair crimped and used copious amounts of hairspray to achieve the volume, especially in her bangs. Blue eyeliner ringed her eyes, and today she wore a Bon Jovi T-shirt and legwarmers over her jeans.

"Good morning," I said, smiling. Besides her being a caricature of a long-ago decade with a tendency to be a little ditzy, she knew herbs almost better than Bonnie. I enjoyed her company immensely and if I ever wanted any friends, she'd be at the top of my list.

"Did you know they were playing Def Leopard on the oldies station today?" she asked as she set her bag behind the counter. "Like, what kind of nonsense is that?"

I didn't answer, but instead returned to my dusting.

"It's just a travesty, if you ask me. I mean, that's the best music. It should be played on the regular station, not the oldies. That's for, like, *old* people."

I didn't bother to point out she was in her fifties, whether she liked it or not. No, we weren't old, but we weren't young, either. That's why they called it middle age.

She flipped through the calendar. "Oh! Monica's coming in today! I wonder if that comfrey soap helped with her acne. I'd better figure out a plan D if it didn't."

Monica, a local teen in town, had one of the worst cases of acne I'd seen in my life. After being to four different dermatologists in the surrounding area and being given some pretty heavy medication with little results, she'd come to Sage Advice. Annabelle had made three different soaps for her. The first three hadn't produced the clear skin she'd strived for, but she had high hopes for the comfrey.

Once I turned the door signage to *open*, the morning progressed very quickly. I helped customers in the front, while Annabelle flitted from the counter to the back room where she worked on our specialty orders.

After a couple hours had passed, she pulled me aside. "Where's Bonnie?"

I checked the clock on the wall. "What does the schedule say?"

"She was supposed to be here an hour ago."

I furrowed my brow, debating what to do. Should I go upstairs and check on her, or let her be for now? It wouldn't be the first instance where she lost track of time.

"Maybe she's not feeling well," Annabelle said. "Let's give her another hour, then we can, like, make sure she's okay."

Glad I wasn't the one to make the call, I got back to work. But we decided it was time to intervene when lunchtime rolled around.

"I'll go check on her," she said as I straightened up one of the display tables. When she returned moments later, she shrugged. "Nothing."

"Was her door unlocked? Did you go inside?"

"Yep. She's, like, not there. Did she tell you about any appointments she may have had?"

I shook my head. "Let me call her." Worry coursed through me as I pulled my phone from my back pocket and dialed. It rang and then went to voicemail. "Hey, Bonnie. Annabelle and I haven't heard from you all morning, which is unusual. Can you give us a call and let us know you're okay?"

After I hung up, Annabelle and I stared at each other a minute, then she said, "Why don't you go get lunch? I'll stay here and wait."

"Do you think we should call the police?"

Annabelle rolled her eyes. "On all the television cop shows they say it's not a missing persons case until twenty-four hours have passed. It's been, like, what… three? Four?"

True. Many, many years ago, Cassie, my character on the soap opera, As the Years Turn, had gone missing. She'd been thrown off a cliff by a jilted lover and barely survived. Frankly, my character had deserved it. In a nutshell, she was a sexy man-eating killer who always got away with murder while running her clothing empire. Her only redeeming quality was that she always stood up for those who couldn't defend themselves. In that particular storyline, the police hadn't come looking for Cassie until twenty-four hours after her disappearance. She'd survived at the bottom of the canyon on berries, fought off a coyote with a tree branch, and sipped water from a pristine stream before they'd found her. The whole sequence of events had taken a month to film, but that was the formula of daytime television—wring out every drop of drama until it's time to move on to the next bombshell.

"Go grab us lunch," Annabelle said. "I'm totally starving."

Actually, I figured a walk and some fresh air would do me good. I ran upstairs and grabbed my purse, then headed out, following the path down to the Riverwalk.

The sound of the rushing river soothed my nerves. A couple of fishermen stood on the other bank, casting their lines. As I strolled along toward the sandwich shop, Subs and Smiles, the stress began to ebb from me. Bonnie would show up eventually. She had an appointment she'd forgotten to tell us about and she'd be rushing in at any moment, or phoning me to apologize.

A man approached me on the pathway. As we got closer, I realized it was Doug, our local homeless drug addict who lived under the bridge up the Riverwalk on the other side of Sage Advice. The first time we'd met, he'd frightened me a little, but coming from Los Angeles, seeing a drug addict out of it on the street wasn't a new sight. The second time I'd met him, he chased me down and handed me the wallet I'd dropped. After that, we'd become somewhat friendly. It was then I learned he was a cousin to our town mayor. Lots of people whispered, wondering how the mayor would allow a family member to live without a roof over his head.

"Hey, Doug," I said, studying his too-thin frame and the ragged clothes on him. "How's it going today?"

"Sam! I'm good, good." His gaze seemed bright, his voice lucid. I doubted he was high.

"I'm headed to Subs and Smiles. Can I grab you anything to eat?"

He grinned and shook his head. "That's nice of you, but no thanks. I'm fine for today."

As we parted ways, I realized he always said that. But what about tomorrow? Or the next day? Between his addiction and lack of nutrition, I did worry that one day he wouldn't be okay, and we'd find him dead under the bridge. Like everyone else, too, I wondered why the dang mayor didn't do something to help his kin.

I'd reached the part of the Riverwalk I adored. No storefronts, just the quiet peace of nature. Standing in the silence, I breathed in the fresh air and listened to the rushing water and the birds. Heywood nourished my cold, aching soul, and once again I couldn't find any guilt in the way I'd left things in my old life.

With a sigh, I glanced over the river once again. Something pink caught my eye down the Riverwalk a few feet, lodged in a thicket of bushes on the shore. Probably a lost hat from one of the many river rafters who floated past. I made my way down the bank to fetch it. No sense leaving garbage in the beautiful, pristine water. As I leaned over to get it, my breath caught in my throat and I scrambled backward until I once again reached the paved walkway.

My body trembled while a scream caught in my throat. I shut my eyes and pinched my arm, hoping I was dreaming. Pain radiated from where I squeezed. No dream. Hard, cold, awful reality.

That pink hat had been resting on the head of my now deceased boss, Bonnie.

CHAPTER 3

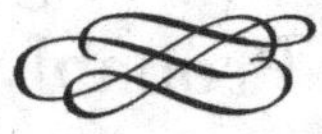

As I stared at the pink hat and waited for the police to arrive, tears streamed down my face. Bonnie had been so kind to me even though she hadn't known me. She'd sensed my desperation and taken me under her wing with a job and a place to live. Her kindness, not only to me, but to others in town, seemed to know no bounds.

And this was how someone had repaid her. Sticking a knife through her sternum and dumping her into a river like garbage to be washed away. Unbelievable.

A group of people led by the head of the river rafting company walked by. Their tour guide prattled on about the history of Heywood, throwing in a few bad jokes every now and then.

When it got too cold for the river rafts to be on the water, the company gave walking tours. I sat on the shore, praying I blocked the view of Bonnie's body. As they disappeared around the bend, I breathed a sigh of relief.

"Hey, there!"

I glanced up to see a woman approaching dressed in a green sheriff's uniform. About five foot three and muscular with short black hair, she grinned as her gaze flitted from the water back to me. I struggled to my feet, the weight of Bonnie's death pressing on me like a tanker truck. "I'm Sheriff Mallory Richards," she said, extending her hand to me. "And you are?"

"Sam Jones," I said, taking her palm in mine.

"And dispatch said you found Bonnie?"

I nodded and pointed to the pink hat barely visible in the bushes.

"Have you touched her?"

"No."

Mallory glanced around. "I've got another deputy coming down as well as the ambulance. It'll take them a long minute to get here, though, since there's not any direct access to this spot on the Riverwalk."

I crossed my arms over my chest, suddenly cold, despite the warm fall air. Talking to the cops wasn't something I wanted to do. After leaving Los Angeles, my plan had been to live a quiet, unassuming life away from the spotlight of Hollywood and the attention of the police. Being in the middle of a murder investigation didn't bode well for such a plan.

"Can you tell me what happened?" Mallory asked, taking a pen and small pad of paper from her breast pocket.

I explained that Bonnie hadn't come to work earlier, but it wasn't something that had us truly worried, so we hadn't called the police. "We didn't want to waste your time," I said. "In case Bonnie did show up."

Mallory nodded and jotted down some notes. "Did she have a habit of being late?"

"Yes. And forgetting to tell us she had an appointment, or even that she was taking the day off. Like I said, we weren't too worried when she didn't show."

"How did you end up here at the Riverwalk?"

"I was going for lunch." Dang it. I should call Annabelle and tell her there wouldn't be any sandwiches, and Bonnie was dead. The task seemed insurmountable. Maybe I should wait and break the news to her in person.

As Mallory studied the area, a couple other

deputies arrived. One young enough to be my son, if I'd ever had any children, the other, in his fifties with salt and pepper hair, a solid build and a nice grin. It surprised me I'd never seen him around town before. But then again, I did keep to myself and rarely ventured beyond Sage Advice, except to jog the Riverwalk.

"This is Deputy Branson," Mallory said, pointing to him. "He's going to finish your interview."

Mallory handed him her pen and pad of paper, walked down to the water's edge, and squatted, staring at Bonnie.

"Jordan Branson," the deputy said, grinning.

"Sam Jones."

"Have we met?"

I shook my head, certain I'd remember those green eyes if we had.

"Strange. You look familiar to me."

He didn't seem like the type who would enjoy a daytime soap opera, and I pivoted the conversation. No sense continuing a discussion I didn't want to have. "I need to get back to the store."

"Of course. And where do you work? How did you find the deceased?"

With a sigh, I repeated everything that had

happened that morning. Jordan nodded and took notes.

"I'm sorry," he said. I met his gaze as the EMTs rolled a gurney down the pathway. "It's tough losing a friend."

Tears welled in my eyes as I considered all the losses I'd suffered the past three months. My husband, my friend and boss, and my former life. "Thanks." Clearing my throat, I didn't meet his gaze. "Can I go now?"

"Just a couple more questions. Did you see anyone around here before you found the deceased?"

"Yes. Doug."

He arched an eyebrow at me. "The homeless guy who lives under the bridge up that way?"

I nodded as he pointed over my shoulder.

"Where did you see him?"

"Back that way a bit," I replied. "He was headed toward the bridge."

"Did he say anything to you?"

"I offered to get him a sandwich and he politely declined."

"That was nice of you."

With a shrug, I said, "I like to think I'm a nice person most of the time."

He chuckled as a sinking feeling settled in my

stomach. Had I just thrown Doug under the proverbial bus? I'd been so focused on getting back to the store, it hadn't occurred to me I'd served him up on a silver platter.

"He didn't have anything to do with it," I said quickly, trying to cover my tracks. "Doug wouldn't hurt anyone."

Jordan smiled. "We'll still have to question him anyway. Do you know anyone who would want to hurt Bonnie?"

The scene in the store yesterday replayed in my mind. Doctor Garrett Butte had been anything but happy with Bonnie, but did that mean he'd killed her? I didn't want to give the sheriff's office anymore ammunition. I didn't want to be involved.

But what if Butte had killed Bonnie? I owed her so much, I had to make the police aware of their argument... and the fact Bonnie had said it hadn't been the first one.

"Garrett Butte was in the store yesterday, yelling at Bonnie."

"About what?"

"One of his patients came in to see her and Bonnie gave her some herbal remedies. He was angry that they worked better than his pharmaceuticals, and that she'd tampered with his patient's treatment."

Jordan furrowed his brow. "But the patient sought out Bonnie by herself, correct?"

"Yes."

"So there wasn't really any tampering with the doctor/patient relationship."

"I agree, but that's not the way Butte saw it."

As Jordan scribbled more notes, I longed to go back to bed and start the day over. Although Bonnie's murder hurt me almost as much as my husband's had, I couldn't help wondering what my next steps were. What happened to the store? My apartment? Would I be forced to start all over again?

"Are you going to be okay?" Jordan asked. "You look really pale."

The tears started again, but I nodded and tried to swallow past them. No such luck. They streamed down my cheeks like a waterfall. I hadn't yet come to terms with my husband's killing, and someone else I cared about had died violently. "It's... I've had a rough day," I whispered.

"Yes, you have. Can I drive you back to Sage Advice?"

I shook my head. "I'd prefer to walk." I needed time to process finding Bonnie.

"Are you sure?"

"Yes. Can I go now?"

"Let me check with the sheriff."

As he strode over to her, I studied him out of the corner of my eye. Confident. Self-assured. While he spoke to the sheriff, he placed his hands on his hips and nodded in a deferring manner, showing he respected his boss.

A moment later, he returned to my side. "She said you can go now, but we'll probably be around soon to have another chat." He almost sounded apologetic. "Are you sure I can't drive you back?"

"I'm fine. Thank you." Turning from him, I strode away, down the Riverwalk. The water rushing by now seemed deafening, and I wished those stupid birds would shut up. Between my worry for the future, my deep sadness over Bonnie, and the natural sounds around me, it was all deafening—too much for me. My head seemed to be buzzing so loudly, I wanted to tear my hair out and scream at the top of my lungs to drown out the sounds.

I broke into a run and hurried back to the store where I found Annabelle behind the counter, the phone up to her ear.

"There you are!" she yelled. "Like, I've been

calling and calling… Bonnie still hasn't shown up… I'm don't know what to do!"

"Bonnie's dead," I said, crying once again. "She was murdered."

Annabelle stared at me a long moment, her eyes wide as if she were trying to decide if I had lost my mind. "Is this some type of joke? Because, like, if it is, I'm not laughing, Sam."

"It's not a joke. I found her. She was in the river with a knife in her heart."

As Annabelle slowly brought her hand to her mouth and swayed where she stood, I hoped she didn't topple over.

"What… how? Who did it?"

I shrugged. "I have no idea."

"Who would do such a thing? I mean, Bonnie was sweet most of the time, but she had a mean streak, too. Would someone want to kill her because of it?"

"You'd know better than me. I've only been here three months. I've never seen her be mean to anyone. Someone wanted her dead."

"Oh, my goodness," she said, slowly sinking onto the stool behind the counter. "What… I don't know what to do."

"The cops will be by to talk to you."

She groaned, then shot to her feet and hurried

over to me, throwing her arms around my neck. As her body began to tremble, I slowly hugged her back.

It had been a long time since I'd experienced a human touch that included deep emotion, and the sensation felt foreign to me. Comforting, yet awkward. As we stood in the middle of Sage Advice, both of us crying and attempting to console each other, I now worried for our futures.

When the door chimes rang, we turned to see who had entered. A woman I didn't recognize strode in, but said nothing as her critical gaze roamed the store. Tall, thin, and maybe a few years younger than me, she wore her blonde hair swept up in a messy bun, her long legs clad in a pair of jeans. A cardigan sweater covered her thin arms, a white T-shirt underneath.

"Can we help you?" Annabelle asked, wiping her cheeks with her fingertips.

"I'm looking for my mother," the woman replied.

Glancing around the store searching for a customer I must have missed when I entered, I had no idea who she could've possibly meant. Based on the confusion on Annabelle's face, she had no idea, either. Except for us, Sage Advice was empty.

"There hasn't been anyone in the store for about a half-hour," Annabelle said. "Can you tell me what she looks like and I'll see if I can remember her being here?"

With a deep sigh, the woman rolled her eyes. "Bonnie. I'm looking for Bonnie."

Annabelle and I exchanged glances. It didn't surprise me I wasn't aware Bonnie had a child. I'd only been around a short period of time and Bonnie had never mentioned her. But Annabelle could do nothing to hide her shock even if she tried.

"What?!" she screeched. "Bonnie's your *mother*?!"

"Yes. Now can you go tell her Catherine is here? I must speak to her."

Oh, no.

How did we break the news that her mother was dead?

CHAPTER 4

DID we tell her to go to the police? Or just blurt out the painful information and not bother to sugarcoat it?

"Bonnie never told me she had a daughter," Annabelle said, narrowing her gaze on the stranger. "What about you, Sam?"

I shook my head, still too stunned to speak.

"We weren't close," Catherine muttered. "Can you please fetch her for me?"

"Where do you live?" Annabelle asked. "I haven't seen you around town."

Catherine crossed her arms over her chest and glared at us. "Phoenix. I live in Phoenix. What is this? I answer forty questions and I gain the magical key that gives me access to my mother?"

"She's not here," I replied, still unsure if I should deliver the news or allow the police to do so.

"Sam, can I talk to you a minute?" Annabelle said. "In the back room?"

Relieved to be getting out of the uncomfortable situation, I followed her.

"What are we going to do?" Annabelle hissed. "I never knew she had a daughter. Not *once* did Bonnie mention her. What if she's the murderer pretending to be Bonnie's daughter in the hopes of taking all her assets?"

Her theory sounded like something out of my soap opera. "I think we just need to tell her the truth," I whispered. "If Bonnie never spoke of her, my guess is they were estranged."

"Maybe we should say Bonnie was involved in an accident and the police would have more information."

A solid idea and not a total lie. Bonnie had indeed suffered a terrible accident.

"Excuse me?" Catherine called from the front room. "Where is my mommy dearest? She's usually tucked away upstairs in her little hovel, or in the back room grinding down plants. This shouldn't be a hard question for you to answer!"

"Let's tell her the truth and send her over to the police," I said. "Get her out of the store."

Annabelle nodded. "Okay, you do the talking."

Taking a deep breath, I threw my shoulders back and strode out to the front. In the short time she'd been in the store, Catherine had proved to be rude and condescending. If she were my daughter, I wouldn't want to have anything to do with her, either.

I smiled as I approached. "The reason we're so hesitant to speak to you about Bonnie is, first of all, she's never mentioned you."

"You don't believe I'm her daughter?"

"That's not for me to decide," I replied. *Get her out of the store.* "But Bonnie was killed this morning. For further details, you'll have to go to the police."

The woman's eyes widened, and I waited for the tears. My own mother and I had had our differences, but it still hurt when she'd passed away.

"How was she killed?" Catherine asked, not a drop of sympathy in her voice. "Car accident? Did she fall?"

I shook my head. "She was found down by the

river caught up in a thicket of bushes. She was murdered."

As Catherine crossed her arms over her chest and began pacing the store, I once again looked for any signs of sorrow, and found none.

"So she got what she deserved," Catherine said, almost in a whisper.

"No, she didn't," Annabelle shot back. "I don't know what your problem was with her, but people liked Bonnie."

Catherine whipped around, her gaze blazing with fury. "If no one saw through her charade, that's their fault. She was a terrible human being."

"That's not the person we knew!" Annabelle shouted. I'd never heard her raise her voice, let alone confront someone. Her passion for protecting Bonnie surprised me.

I didn't want to hear the drama of Catherine's supposed awful past with her mother. I didn't think she was lying because I believed everyone had something or someone in their past that didn't sit well with them. Be it a regret or a grudge, it didn't matter. But there was no need for a scene and for her to reveal the details of how Bonnie had wronged her. Catherine had to leave so Annabelle and I could attempt to figure out what our next steps would be.

"The best thing for you to do is to go speak to the police," I said. "They can give the details we simply don't have."

Catherine glared at me, then glanced around the store again. "I may have hated Bonnie, but we had an agreement where she'd leave everything to me." Her gaze met mine and a slow smile spread across her face. "I guess I'm your new boss."

Annabelle groaned and cursed under her breath.

Oh, heck no. I didn't want to work for this woman. Her toxicity spread faster than the stench of her perfume. Besides, if she wasn't in contact with Bonnie, how would she know she now owned the store?

With ease, I slipped into my Cassie character. Calm. Self-assured. She'd never tolerate this woman, and I had no intention of doing so either. I strode up to Catherine so mere inches separated us. "Here's what I would suggest. Go to the police. Find out what they can tell you about your mother's demise. Act at least a little bit upset about it because you'll win points with everyone in town. And finally, never, ever assume *anything*. If you were my daughter, I wouldn't leave you my trash, let alone my store."

Her nostrils flared as her cheeks reddened. But I wasn't done quite yet.

"Until you can prove you do indeed own this store, you're no longer welcome here. If the time comes, we'll hand over the keys. Now, please go before I call the cops and have them take you in for impersonating the kin of a dead woman."

I had no idea if that was even a crime, but seeing her faltering gaze, Catherine wondered the same. She turned to leave.

As the bells on the door sounded, I shut my eyes and sighed with relief. Hopefully, I'd scared her away until Annabelle and I found out the truth, or at least had an inkling of what was going on.

"Oh, my goodness," Annabelle said. "It's you. It's truly you."

Uh oh. I didn't like the sound of that.

"You're... you're Cassie. I'd recognize the haughty voice anywhere."

Could this day get any worse? How in the world did I get a job with probably the only person in town who watched the soap opera? I turned and smiled. "I have no idea what you're talking about."

She shook her head. "Nope. You aren't going to fool me. I see it all too clearly. You're

Samantha Rathbone, daytime actress extraordinaire, who disappeared from the face of the Earth."

I threw my head back and laughed. "Annabelle, you're wrong. Don't say such ridiculous things."

"When you first got here, I about had a heart attack the first time I saw you. Like, Samantha Rathbone in the little town of Heywood working at Sage Advice? Your face was all bruised up and your hair curly, not straight like on the show… you wore glasses… and you didn't act like I thought a Hollywood actress should. I wanted to ask you about it a million times, but I was sure I was wrong."

"Annabelle, I—"

"I've been watching you since you first joined *As the Years Turn* twenty years ago. So please, just stop denying it. I'm not going to tell anyone."

The gig was up for me, my lies exposed.

I turned to her, sighing in defeat. "Okay, you're right. But please, don't say anything."

She hurried over to me and took my hand in hers. "What in the world happened? The last I saw on the news, no one knew if you were alive or dead!"

"Well, as you can see, I'm alive."

"Did your husband really do those things? Did he steal all that money?"

I nodded. His actions had not only led to his death, but to me being blacklisted from Hollywood. "He did. I had no idea about any of it."

And that had bothered me since the moment I discovered the truth of his business dealings. How had I missed the immense amount of stress he'd been under? How had I not been aware the police had been questioning him for months? Sometimes I felt we'd grown so far apart, I hadn't seen the signs right in front of me. Either that, or he was a better actor than me.

"Why didn't you tell anyone you were alive?" Annabelle asked. "Wouldn't your friends in Hollywood want to know?"

"It's complicated," I said. "But no, they don't care if I'm alive or dead, and that's okay with me. After the whole fiasco, I wanted to start over, to live a quiet life in a little town where no one recognized me."

Annabelle nodded as she slowly studied my face. "You know, you're a very pretty woman, but you *do* look different than you did on television. Your hair is curly, you wear glasses, and barely any makeup. I guess without all the fancy clothing and layers of makeup Samantha Rathbone wore, you do look like a different person."

I didn't bother to mention I'd also left behind the hair dye, as well as the Botox and fillers the studio had insisted I shoot into my face. Heaven forbid I look like the fifty-four-year-old woman I was.

"Okay, Sam Jones. Your secret is safe with me. I'm not going to mention who you really are to anyone."

"Thank you, Annabelle," I said. "I appreciate you respecting my privacy."

"Do you know how they killed you off the show?"

I'd wondered, but never actually watched the episode. Even though I wanted a quiet existence, I was still hurt and angry over what had taken place to end my flashy, large life. "I'm sure it wasn't nice."

She laughed and shook her head. "They had Barron kill you off by knocking you over the head with one of your 14th century Chinese vases, which happened to contain jewelry his wife wore while alive."

It made sense. In the last scene I'd shot before my life went up in flames, both literally and figuratively, my character's former lover, Barron, had accused me of killing his wife, which my character had done earlier in the year. It had been a blowout fight, including me slapping him, which I had to admit, I enjoyed because I disliked my co-star. With the magic of editing, they could've taken past scenes and pieced together something resembling my death. Yet, I had to chuckle at the absurdity of it all.

"Then Barron set your house on fire," Annabelle continued. "I stopped watching after that."

How poetic. My then real-life house that I'd shared with my embezzler husband, Gerald, had been razed by the summer fires just as I was leaving Hollywood, and that's why people thought I may be dead.

I smiled, even though sadness enveloped me. I'd been wronged by Hollywood and it still caused me pain.

"Honestly, I'm glad you're here, Sam," Annabelle said. "I'm glad we're friends."

Just like that, I felt slightly lighter. Despite me keeping my distance from most people, my working relationship with Annabelle had always felt authentic, unlike any friendship I'd ever had in Hollywood.

"And I promise you, no one will find out who you are from me."

"Thanks."

She glanced over my shoulder at the door and winced.

"What's wrong?" I whispered.

"The reporter for the *Heywood Sentinel* is here, and he's as nosey as they come. You may not have a secret for much longer."

"Are you kidding me?" I hissed as I turned around. Really... could this day get any worse? What more could possibly go wrong?

The last thing I wanted was to speak to the press, even if it was the reporter for the *Heywood Sentinel*. Granted, I was used to dealing with the likes of *Vanity Fair* and *People,* but the little, round man with the bald head and beady eyes could do me more harm than he knew. I fought the urge to scream at the top of my lungs.

"I'm looking for Sam Jones," he said. "I was told she worked here."

For a brief second, I debated telling him Sam Jones wasn't in the store, but figured it would backfire on me at some point once he discovered the truth. "What can I do for you?"

"I wanted to talk about the murder," he said,

almost breathlessly, a slow smile spreading across his face. Was he excited by the killing? Probably. It must be difficult to be a reporter in a town where the front-page news consisted of a tractor being stuck on the highway or the school's bake sale.

"I think that's something you should discuss with the police," I said.

"But you found Bonnie, and you also work here. You've got the big scoop for me!"

"How did you know I found her?" I asked.

"A reporter always has eyes and ears in the police station," he said, winking.

That may be so, but I didn't appreciate his mole throwing out my name. My quiet, innocuous life seemed to be unraveling by the second. "I have no comment."

"Oh, come on," he said, rolling his eyes. "You found a body. Of course you have a comment. Tell me the details. What happened after you found her? Tell me what you felt when you did. Were you disgusted? Surprised?"

I stared at the little man a long time before answering, my anger boiling. What was it with reporters? Why were they so horribly obnoxious? Was it genetics? Something they learned at school? There didn't seem to be any difference between this guy and anyone at the large magazines. "Do you realize someone I cared for very much has died? I felt absolute heartbreak when I found her. I cried, and I was horrified. Is that what you're looking for?" Tears welled in my eyes despite my fury. Even this tiny man, both physically and emotionally, couldn't erase the horror and terrible ache of discovering Bonnie's body.

"Tell me more," he said, oblivious to my pain. "Where exactly on the Riverwalk did you find her? How was her body positioned? What did she look like? Do you think she'd been dead long?"

"Get out," I said, pointing at the door. "I have no further comment."

CHAPTER 5

Word spread quickly throughout the town about Bonnie's death. The store almost became unmanageable. Not from people looking to purchase our goods, but those who wanted to gossip and get the scoop directly from me. Annabelle had finally suggested we close early, and I readily agreed.

After retreating to the upstairs around dinnertime, I stopped in Bonnie's apartment and fed her cat, Catnip. The green-eyed, all-black feline meowed and carefully weaved himself in and out of my legs. When I tried to leave, he followed. I finally slipped out of the apartment without him, but he stood at the door and cried. What could I do? Leaving him alone wasn't an option. No one would be by to fetch him, unless that wretched Catherine really did now own all of Bonnie's things. In that case, I couldn't imagine her taking kindly to Catnip, and he'd probably end up in the shelter. I wouldn't allow that. After entering Bonnie's place again, I grabbed all of Catnip's food and bowls, a few toys, and brought them back to my place. Then, I fetched Catnip himself.

I'd never had a cat—well, unless one counted the feral one I sort of adopted when I was young —but how hard could it be to care for one? Growing up poor on the streets of Oakland, I'd shared bits and pieces of my meals with my feline friend I'd named Frank. My mom, a barely-functioning alcoholic, had forbidden me from bringing any animal into our home. When I went out on my own, I couldn't afford to take care of anyone else, and when I landed my role on *As the Years Turn*, my focus had been solely on my career. Looking back, it all seemed so empty and depressing, even though I'd convinced myself that working twelve-hour days and attending fundraisers and parties most nights was a fulfilling life.

"You're going to be staying with me for now," I

said, setting up his bowls in the corner of the kitchen. "Let's do our best to get along, okay?"

He jumped to the back of the couch and curled up while staring out the window. Did he know Bonnie wasn't returning? If not, he'd figure it out, and I imagined he'd be more upset than me. I'd deal with it when the time came.

I made some chamomile tea and sat down with a loud groan. What an awful day. Of course, the big questions on everyone's mind had been, who killed Bonnie and why? I had no answers. Bonnie had always been kind to me. .I'd never seen this mean streak both Annabelle and Catherine mentioned, but again, I'd only been in town for three months. Perhaps, as time went by, I would have witnessed it.

As an outsider looking in, I saw four suspects. First, Doctor Butte. Could he have been upset enough to kill Bonnie? Possibly. If what she said was true and he was one of those horrible doctors who kept their patients just sick enough to keep returning, then yes. He'd want the person responsible for actually healing his patients gone. If he didn't deal with Bonnie, word would get around that she could help people when he couldn't... or wouldn't. His income would take a significant hit.

However, Bonnie indicated Butte had been angry at her for years. Why kill her now? Why not two years ago? Had he simply reached his limit?

Speaking of limits, then there was Catherine. Ugh. What a nasty woman. If Bonnie and her daughter had been estranged, Bonnie had obviously reached her limit with her. I had to assume though that if Catherine had been the one to cut off her mother, Bonnie would still discuss her daughter, even if it was to share the heartbreak that situation caused. Could they have had a fight and Catherine stabbed her? Or, if Bonnie had left everything to her, then she also had a monetary motive... if Bonnie actually had anything. I had no idea about her financial situation. Did she own the building? How much were the assets in the store worth? Did she have any investments? That would be something the police would investigate.

Which, unfortunately, led me to Annabelle. I hated to consider it, but she was the one who mentioned that Catherine could be pretending to be her daughter in hopes of taking Bonnie's assets. A far-reaching plan, but an interesting one nonetheless. However, it also made me question if Annabelle was trying to set up Catherine to take the fall for Bonnie's death. What if Annabelle had killed Bonnie for reasons unknown to me? Then, Catherine entered the store and Annabelle fingered her as the perfect patsy.

I assumed the police would also investigate Doug, the homeless man who lived down by the river under the bridge. He had been in the area and I'd mentioned it to the police. Guilt washed through me, causing me nausea despite the soothing chamomile tea. Everyone knew they could easily pin the murder on him and he'd really have no way to fight back.

When Catnip nuzzled my neck under my hair, I startled, having forgotten he was around. I closed my eyes as he burrowed through my thick curls, his purring relaxing me. Maybe that was why Bonnie had given him that name. Catnip was a potent herb for relaxation, and he certainly seemed to have that effect on me.

I couldn't help but wonder: if my character, Cassie, on *As the Years Turn* had killed Bonnie, how would she have done it? Probably with a poisoned tea. She'd usually saved the violent deaths for men. And what would be her motives? Definitely money. If Cassie thought she'd been financially wronged, she'd eliminate the perpetrator. Or, if someone had hurt anybody she cared about, she'd off them, depending on the offense. I'd spent hours upon hours with the writers of *As the Years Turn* going over scenarios for Cassie, along with motives and methods for her killing. Although our plots were always a bit over the top for dramatic purposes, we still had to be clever, and that required a lot of imagination. I'd probably given too much thought to being a murderer during my time on the soap opera, and that now seemed to have bled into my real life.

The one thing that bothered me the most was the press sniffing around. Someone in the police force had shared with them that I'd discovered the body. Of course, they'd want details. However, I wanted to keep my name out of the paper and not draw attention to myself. Could I trust Annabelle to keep my secret? Yes... as long as she wasn't the killer. If so, all bets were off. If she murdered Bonnie, her moral compass was wonky to begin with and her letting everyone know who I used to be was the least of my worries.

Catnip raised his head and jumped down onto the couch beside me, staring at the front door, his ears twitching. Was he waiting for Bonnie? When he began to pace, I said, "Your food's in the kitchen." The glare he gave me conveyed something like, "I'm not stupid. You are. Guess again about what I want."

I realized I'd left his litterbox at Bonnie's. "I'm sorry," I said. "Do you have to use the bathroom? Let me grab it for you. How rude of me, Catnip."

After hurrying next door, I glanced around Bonnie's place and didn't see the litterbox. Since her apartment mirrored mine, it didn't take long to check each room. Where in the world did Catnip go to the bathroom?

On the desk in her bedroom lay some papers. No. It wouldn't be right for me to go through them. The police would most likely be around soon to do a thorough investigation of her apartment and I didn't want to leave any fingerprints. I should leave the investigating to them. But what harm would it do if I just glanced at them?

Cameras. I would forever be searching for cameras in any room because in Hollywood, I'd lived with them filming my every move without even knowing about it. My former husband's set up had been quite elaborate. I searched the ceiling for something similar, although I had a hard time believing Bonnie would have wanted cameras in her home. She struck me as someone who cherished her privacy.

When I didn't see anything remotely resembling a lens, I quickly rifled through the papers in the dim light, using the tip of my nail move them around. Darkness had settled outside, but the streetlight provided enough illumination for me to see.

The power bill. She'd paid off the mortgage on the building... impressive. A request for her to speak at the high school to some students thinking of going into the medical field. I scanned the letter. Doctor Butte would also be speaking that day, and they hoped the herbalist and the medical practitioner would help give the kids a well-rounded, thought-provoking seminar. I snorted at the idea. From what I'd seen, Bonnie and Butte went together like kerosene and fire. Those poor kids would most likely be subjected to a screaming match like the one I'd witnessed.

With a sigh, I turned to leave. As I passed by the kitchen, hands pressed into my back and pushed me down into the living room. My face barely missing the coffee table as my hands hit the rug. I curled up, prepared to be assaulted. Relief flooded through me when footsteps clamored down the stairs and out the back door, not through the storefront. I stared at the carpet for a moment while on all fours, listening for any other sounds while my anger simmered. When had someone broken into Bonnie's apartment? Had they been here the whole time I was inside? And if so, why not wait quietly until I left? Maybe my attacker had been afraid I'd discover them? I had been mere feet away when they pushed me.

When I was certain I was alone, I slowly stood. Should I call the police? Yes. Would I be in trouble for being in Bonnie's apartment? Maybe. I didn't want any hassle, but they needed to be aware someone had been here. I felt my back pocket for my phone, but realized I'd left it on my kitchen counter. First, I'd head downstairs to check the back door and make sure the store was okay. Then, I'd call the police. But I remembered why I came into Bonnie's apartment to begin with. The litterbox.

I glanced around the apartment once again. Where in the world did the cat go to the bathroom?

Hurrying down the stairs, I didn't find anything out of the ordinary. Our back-room work-space remained untouched. The door leading out to the back, however, had been jimmied open, the frame destroyed.

With a slew of curses, I walked out the front

of the store and headed around the side of the building. I was able to move the dumpster in front of the door, and then I locked the squeaky wheels in place. Yes, someone else could certainly move it to get in, but at least I'd hear them wrestling with the thing.

Returning inside, I locked up the front once again and headed up the stairs. As I opened the door to my own place, I glanced around in case I'd been mistaken in thinking I was alone, my heart thundering. I heard nothing out of the ordinary, so I hurried inside to the kitchen and grabbed a knife from the drawer. The thought of stabbing someone curled my stomach, but the blade was the only weapon I had. I carefully moved through the apartment, finding no one in the bedroom or living room. The closets were clear. I crept toward the bathroom, both anger and fear clenching my chest. If someone was in my space, could I stab them?

When a sound emanated from the bathroom, I almost gasped and gave myself away. Instead, I clenched my teeth and raised my knife, stepping around the corner.

To find Catnip, perched on the toilet seat. He glared at me, meowed loudly, then jumped down.

To my utter shock, he'd been using the toilet. He didn't need a litterbox.

I leaned against the doorframe and laughed, a reaction to the stress of the day and to seeing a cat relieving himself like a human. Leave it to Bonnie to teach her cat to use the bathroom.

CHAPTER 6

THE NEXT MORNING, I opened the store as usual and drank copious amounts of coffee. Every little sound had woken me during the night, and each time I rose from my bed to investigate, I found Catnip doing cat things, like chasing a toy across the floor or parkouring in my living room. While he now rested quietly upstairs, I waited for the police to arrive. The previous night when I'd called, I'd been told that if I didn't feel my life was in danger, they'd be by the next morning. I found it odd, but chalked it to small town policing.

Deputy Jordan Branson strode in right at ten. As he approached the counter grinning, I couldn't help but think that, in Hollywood, he'd be cast as the lead detective in a cop show. His character would be played as a fair man to his people, liked by all in the department. But his wife would leave him because of his dedication to his job, and she'd be unaware of the affair he had with one of his female supervisors. He didn't want his marriage to end and a horrible accident on the job would make his wife realize she still loved him. They'd have a second go at staying together. But depending on how many seasons the show went, he'd somehow screw it up again.

"Ms. Jones," he greeted me. "Is it a good time to tell me what happened last night?"

"Sure. I was frankly a little surprised no one came out when I called."

"Understandable," he said, sighing. "As you know, we're a small department. There was a tractor trailer incident on the highway a few miles up, and it was all hands on deck. Two people died, three went to the hospital."

Yikes. "That's awful. I hadn't heard about it." Studying his face, I now saw the exhaustion of being up most of the night—the stubble on his chin, the bags under his eyes. "Are the three people in the hospital going to make it?"

He shrugged. "I'm not sure. I haven't received any updates. I went home at dawn, slept a few hours, and came here."

"Well, I appreciate you stopping by. Would you like some coffee? Tea?"

"Coffee would be great, thank you. I feel like there isn't enough coffee in the world to get me through this day."

I chuckled as I strode into the back room. "I was just thinking the same thing," I called over my shoulder.

As I set down the steaming mug in front of him, he pulled out a pad of paper and a pen. "Why don't you tell me what happened last night?"

While I repeated my story, I made sure to express I was concerned about Catnip and I hadn't gone into Bonnie's apartment to snoop. Even though my invasion of her space had a dual function, I relayed someone had to take care of her cat.

"That's really nice of you," he said.

"Any decent human being would take him in," I said, shrugging. But if Catnip didn't start sleeping through the night, we may have to make other arrangements. "And when I grabbed him and some of his stuff and returned to my apartment, I realized I hadn't taken the litter box, so I went back. While I was looking for it, someone pushed me from behind."

Jordan furrowed his brow in worry. "Were you hurt?"

"No." I held out my hands. "Just a little rug burn." I'd already applied Calendula salve to facilitate a faster healing.

"Do you think that person was in there the first time you were in Bonnie's apartment?"

"I have no idea."

"Did you see them? Recognize anything about them? Could you tell if they were male or female?"

"I'm sorry, but no. They completely caught me by surprise."

"How odd," he muttered, jotting down some notes. "Either someone was in there when you grabbed the cat the first time, or they entered after you took the cat and before you went back for the litterbox. How much time do you think passed between your visits?"

Taking a long sip of my brew, I thought for a moment. "Maybe a half hour? Forty-five minutes?"

"So, plenty of time for someone to slip in."

Then I remembered the odd way Catnip had been staring at the door. I'd thought he needed to use the bathroom, but perhaps he'd heard something I couldn't... like someone entering Bonnie's apartment.

I relayed the information to Deputy Branson, who noted the timing.

"Based on the cat, you were alone the first time you went in, but not the second."

And that meant someone had seen me going through Bonnie's papers. I reminded myself that just because I had glanced at a few things didn't mean they could link me to the murder.

"You're lucky," he said. "That could've been a bad situation for you. Whoever it was didn't want to kill you, or they would have."

"I agree. I had no idea I wasn't alone." Just saying the words caused a chill to run down my spine.

Two other cops strode in, their faces lined with exhaustion, just like Jordan's. "They're here to do a search on Bonnie's place, as well as the store."

"Sure. Of course."

"They'll also need to look at your apartment."

I met Jordan's gaze and noted the apology in his eyes. Having been through a police search before while living in Los Angeles, I bristled at the idea. It had been a complete violation that time, and I couldn't imagine it being any different now.

"Why? I had nothing to do with what happened to Bonnie."

"She owned the building, so we have to search the whole thing for evidence, including your apartment. The judge issued the warrant for the building in its entirety, not just Bonnie's apartment."

"Am I a suspect?"

Jordan shrugged. "Right now, everyone who knew Bonnie is a suspect."

I swallowed past the bile rising in my throat. Flashbacks of my previous entanglement with law enforcement resurfaced. Even though I'd done nothing wrong then, they still treated me as if I had.

"We'll be gentle with your things," he continued. "If it'll make you feel better, you can come stand in the doorway and watch."

After taking a sip of my coffee, I nodded.

"Let's start in the back room," Jordan said, pointing the police to the doorway behind me. "And pay special attention to the back door. Let's see if we can get prints off it."

A dual investigation to discover who killed Bonnie and who had broken into her apartment and assaulted me. I appreciated the efficiency, and I wondered if the same person had committed both crimes.

"Can you take me through what happened again upstairs?" Jordan asked. "Walk me through your movements?"

"Sure."

As we turned to follow the other officers into the back room, Annabelle came in through the front door. "Sam! Sam! What's going on?!"

Today, she wore a neon pink and green track suit with a matching hair bandana. Where in the world did she shop to find these vintage items? Or maybe they were leftovers from her youth?

"It's okay, Annabelle," I said. "The police just want to do a quick search."

I hadn't mentioned the break-in to her for one simple reason: I didn't trust her. There was a chance Annabelle could've murdered Bonnie. For what reason, I wasn't quite sure, but the incidents in my recent past had given me horrible trust issues. I adored Annabelle, but I also wanted to remain alive and safe. Until I knew she had nothing to do with the murder or the break-in, I'd keep my thoughts on Bonnie's death to myself.

As I climbed the stairs with Deputy Branson behind me, I also remembered our run in with the press the prior day. Now, I wouldn't compare the Hollywood press to the little man of the *Hey-*

wood Sentinel, but he had seemed pretty determined to get a good story. What if he'd been the
one to break into Bonnie's apartment?

"A man was here. I didn't catch his name. He
said he was from the *Heywood Sentinel* and was
quite… pushy."

"Looking for the big story?" Deputy Branson
asked as we reached the landing.

"Yes." I turned to him and crossed my arms
over my chest. "He said he got my name from
someone in the police department."

Branson winced. "Heck. That shouldn't have
happened."

"I agree."

"I'm sorry about that," he sighed. "Heywood's
a small town with not a lot going on. Unfortunately, the sheriff isn't as skilled in murder investigations as she should be, and neither is the
staff."

"Does that include you?"

He shook his head. "I'm a transplant. A cop in
Chicago in a former life. I've worked plenty of
murders."

Interesting. "You came from Chicago to Heywood? That's quite the change."

"Yes. Yes, it was."

I longed to ask a few more questions, but I

didn't want to open up the conversation to me revealing my life prior to Heywood. "That's Bonnie's place," I said, pointing to the door on my left. "And this is mine."

"Is the cat in there?"

"Yes."

"Okay. Is there a way for you to crate it or something while we search?"

"I'll just hold him."

As I opened the door, Catnip jumped from the couch and hurried over to introduce himself to the new guy. I scooped him up as the other cops joined Deputy Branson on the landing.

"We'll split up and do both apartments at once," he said, grinning. "That way, we'll get out of your hair much quicker." He really did seem like a decent human, something I hadn't experienced with my recent dealings with LA law enforcement.

Catnip purred in my arms as the men entered Bonnie's. We stood in the doorway while they conducted their search, which didn't take long in the small space. Nervous butterflies tickled my belly as they picked through the stack of papers I'd glanced at last night. When the police scooped them up and put them in a bag, I turned away and paced the small landing with Catnip.

I heard the others rummaging through my private space. Clenching my teeth, I tried to prepare myself for a horrible mess, just like I had last time my house had been searched.

"Did you and Bonnie keep your doors locked?" Branson asked.

I shook my head. "Neither of us did. We were here all day long. It seemed pointless. She was also up and down the stairs constantly, always hurrying up here to grab something or other, or to check on Catnip."

He nodded, then entered my apartment.

Once again, I paced the landing, my ire growing with each step. I hated strangers in my apartment, touching my things, especially since I'd done nothing wrong.

They'd left Bonnie's door open and I peeked inside to see what the damage was. Stepping over the threshold, I glanced around while Catnip meowed. I felt bad taking him back into his house… like I was somehow teasing him. To my surprise, I couldn't tell anyone had been in Bonnie's apartment—not a thing out of place. Either the Los Angeles police had been especially rough, or the Heywood police had no idea what they were doing.

"We're done here," Branson said as he came

out onto the landing a few moments later. "I'm really sorry for the intrusion."

I glanced into my apartment. They'd left it just as neat as Bonnie's, which pleased me. However, I still couldn't get past the idea of strangers touching my things. As they filed out down the stairs, I tried to ignore them while placing Catnip into my apartment and closing the door.

"Good luck with the investigation," I replied, and followed him down the stairs.

"Do you two need help fixing the back door?" the deputy asked as Annabelle hurried over next to me.

I had no idea how to repair it, but Annabelle shook her head. "We'll take care of it."

The store was busier than usual, and as I walked around and asked people if they needed any assistance, I realized that most weren't buyers. They were in the store hoping to catch a bit of news about Bonnie's murder.

An hour later, when most of them had gone home, Annabelle had already repaired the door and I found her in back working on some specialty tinctures.

She closed the amber bottle with a dropper, then pulled a sticker from the box and wrote the customer's name on it, what the tincture was for, and the dosage. "You know, I've been thinking… we should, like, set a couple of tables out front and use them to serve tea. We could put a small stove back here and grab some pastries from Skippity Skones every morning to serve with the tea. It would be another revenue stream for the store."

I'd had the same idea, but my internal radar screamed. How could Annabelle be making future plans unless she knew something about what happened to Bonnie's estate?

CHAPTER 7

Two days passed without any police presence, and it was a nice break. The press, however, was a different story. That little man, who I learned was named Barry, sniffed around the store like a hungry street dog, always asking the same questions. What did the body look like when I found it? Who do I think killed her? Was it a crime of passion? It got to the point where Annabelle and I speculated that he'd committed the murder just to stir up trouble in town and write a good story.

"I'm calling the cops on you, Barry!" Annabelle screamed on the second day of his harassment. "Some guy named Bubba in prison is going to be really happy to see you!"

Besides Barry, our lives were back to normal, except for Bonnie's murder hanging over us like a dark cloud. I still didn't trust Annabelle, especially when she kept rambling on about her plans for the store. Had she brought up her ideas with Bonnie? What had been the outcome? Had Bonnie ignored her, or had she taken the plans into consideration? It was as if Annabelle knew we'd have a job once the investigation had concluded. If Bonnie's daughter was going to inherit the building, she wouldn't be keeping me and Annabelle around. Not after the confrontation we'd had with her.

"How do you know you're going to be working here once all this settles?" I asked as I dusted the display tables and rearranged the products.

She didn't answer for a long moment, but then sighed and set down the bills she'd been counting. Today she wore jeans, a matching jacket, and a Michael Jackson t-shirt, her hair so sprayed, it didn't move when she shook her head. "I *have* to believe it, Sam. Bonnie... she, like, saved my life. Literally. Because of her, I'm here. Then she gave me a job and an opportunity to better myself even further by educating me."

"How did she save your life?" I asked, now intrigued.

"I was in a terrible relationship. He was an abuser, both physically and mentally. I was miserable, but he kept making me feel like all our problems were my fault, and they weren't. He'd gaslight me until I wasn't sure which way was up. I wondered if I was crazy."

How horrible. In my view, men like him should be thrown in prison and left to rot. "I'm sorry to hear that, Annabelle. How did you end up at Sage Advice?"

"My mom was an herbalist and I learned from her. When I heard Bonnie needed help, I came in to apply for a job, and she hired me. She quickly figured out I was in trouble at home, and she let me stay in your apartment."

Interesting that Annabelle's story mirrored mine in that we'd both been desperate for a second chance, desperate to be rescued.

"My husband wasn't too fond of me working. We needed the money, but he preferred me at home waiting on him. One day, I came into work with bruises on my arms, and Bonnie got involved."

"How?" I asked, leaving my spray cleaner and rag on the table as I walked over to the counter.

"She went to our trailer with a shotgun and told Ralph if he ever spoke to me again, she'd put a hole in him and leave him in the woods for the wolves."

Sweet, little old Bonnie? With a shotgun? Had I even known the real woman? "What happened then?"

"Everything was going pretty good, but then Ralph told me he loved me and wanted to get back together with me. I mentioned it to Bonnie, which was a mistake."

"Did she shoot him?" I asked, both terrified and oddly curious about the answer.

"No, she didn't, but she told me I had a choice to make. I either kept my job and forgot about Ralph, or I quit and went back to him. She said she couldn't stand by my side if I went back to an abusive relationship. I'm not going to lie… it was a hard decision. He had a way of getting under my skin, and he was the world's best gaslighter. A real pro."

"I'm glad you decided to choose the job," I replied, relief sweeping through me.

"Me, too. I'd probably be dead by now. Things were getting bad between us. After I left for good, he started dating Gina over at File It Away."

Interesting "Did they marry?"

Annabelle nodded. "Yes. She had a kid right away. I think they were together two years before she kicked him to the curb."

"Sounds like he should've been arrested for laying hands on you. Did you two have kids?"

Even though Annabelle and I had been working together for three months, I kept our conversations out of the personal realm. Honestly, I felt a little bad I didn't know this very important detail of her life.

"No. I got knocked up by someone else shortly after the breakup, but we never married. I have a daughter, Georgette. She's in the Navy."

"Georgette?" I asked. "Is that a family name?"

She giggled. "No. I named her after Boy George."

Ah, yes. The flamboyant singer from the 80s. I should have guessed that. Also one of the nicest people I'd ever met. Frankly, I didn't know whether to laugh or roll my eyes at Annabelle's dedication to a long-ago era.

"But getting back to the store… that's why it's so important to me," Annabelle continued. "Herbalism is my passion. It's the one thing I'm good at. This place represents me turning my life around, going from an abused woman to someone who helps people. It's all I have. This store… it's, like, my anchor."

I understood anchors all too well. My job playing Cassie on *As the Years Turn* was my anchor for two decades. and I still hadn't recovered from the pain of losing the work I'd loved. Some people were lucky enough to find significant others or close friends to anchor them, but others weren't. For Annabelle, it was a building. For me, a fictional character on television. Or maybe it was the job for both of us?

"I wish there was something I could do to make your wish come true," I said, meaning every word. "That somehow the store will keep going on."

"Don't worry. This place will remain open and I'll still be here. I don't know how it's going to happen, but it will all work out in the end."

How could she be so certain? She obviously knew something I didn't.

When the door chime jingled, I turned to see a woman entering. I smiled as she approached, recognizing her as a regular customer whose name I couldn't place. She was about forty with a black pixie haircut and a friendly demeanor. If I remembered correctly, she came in for her daughter, but I couldn't recall the ailment.

"How can we help you?" I asked.

"I was hoping to pick up my daughter's anxiety tincture," she replied, wringing her hands. "I heard about Bonnie, though. And I hate to say this, but I need to know if I can still get the tincture. It's working. She's feeling so much better. And even though I'm so upset about Bonnie, I have to look after my daughter."

"Never fear," Annabelle said. "Sam and I are keeping everything going. Bonnie was the heart and soul of this shop, but we aren't going to let anyone down. I actually just finished up the tincture earlier today. For Tamera, right?"

"Yes," the mother said, sighing in relief. "Thank you."

As Annabelle hurried in back to fetch it, I rang up the total.

"What's going to happen to the store?" she asked.

I wished I had an answer. "We don't know. I'm sure everything will be fine, though." Might as well keep the hope alive like Annabelle did.

The doors chimed again, and I glanced up to find an elderly man. Wearing a tan suit with a bow tie and fedora, he made me smile. Someone had put on their Sunday best to visit the herb shop.

"Here you go!" Annabelle sang. "Tell Tamera I hope she continues to feel better, and if she has any questions, she can give us a call."

After the woman left, Annabelle leaned in and whispered, "See? That's why we *must* stay open. People come from all over the area to visit Sage Advice. Our work is too important."

In the next breath, she announced she was going to grab us a coffee from Cup of Go.

The little man approached the counter, his expression pleasant and warm. "I'm looking for Sam Jones, please."

Oh, no. This couldn't be anything good.

"Can I ask what this is about?"

"A very personal matter. Would you be Ms. Jones?"

I didn't see a way out and nervous butterflies tickled my belly. Another reporter? Probably not. He was too well dressed and frankly, too old. Maybe a retired doctor? "Y-yes."

"My name is Colin Breckshire, III. I represent Bonnie's estate."

Why the heck was he looking for me? "What can I do for you?"

He reached into his inside coat pocket and pulled out an envelope. "I'm here to deliver this letter to you, Ms. Jones. This is part of Bonnie's last will and testament."

There had to be some mistake. "Are you sure this shouldn't go to her daughter? Or someone else? I've only known Bonnie for a short period of time."

He smiled warmly and shook his head. "I'm positive, Ms. Jones. I don't make mistakes. Bonnie and I met a week ago and she gave me this and told me that in case of her death, I was to deliver this to you before the reading of the will because everything hinges on your decision." He placed the letter on the counter between us.

"What does it say?" I asked, eyeing the offending piece of mail. I didn't want to be involved in anything to do with Bonnie's death.

"That's between you and Bonnie."

With that, he turned and walked out of the store. I stared at the letter for a couple more minutes, thoroughly confused. Why was I in Bonnie's will?

With a long sigh, I picked it up and opened it, immediately recognizing Bonnie's handwriting.

. . .

DEAR SAM,

It took me two days to finally recognize you after you walked into my store looking for a job. You've done excellent work keeping a low profile and hiding your true identity. But, I'm old, and with that comes experience in detecting when people aren't being truthful. Annabelle also figured you out simply because she watched your show every single day. Once the bruising on your face cleared, she started asking questions. I did my best to redirect her and keep your secret.

I've followed your case in Los Angeles very closely. You were wronged in a way that still baffles me to this day. I've wanted to question you a hundred times on whether you're petitioning to have your money returned to you. Just because your husband robbed people doesn't mean you should pay the price with your hard-earned cash. It's wrong, and I hope you'll find the strength to fight for what's yours.

The interviews I watched and read about your so-called? friends and co-workers made me ill. I don't think you had a person willing to stick up for you, and that makes me very sad.

Over our time together, I've grown to respect you very much, and possibly even love you a bit like I would a daughter. You don't know this, but I have one. By my choice, we're estranged. If you think your husband has done horrible things, the stories I could tell you about my daughter would curl your toes. Fraud. Embezzlement. Bribery. She's stolen thousands from me. I don't understand how I produced such a monster.

But now, to the point of this letter. My store, Sage Advice, needs to stay in business. This community demands it, especially when we have so-called medical care from the likes of Doctor Butte. There are other reasons why this store must stay open after I'm gone, but those people need to share their stories with you on their own. It's not my place.

Therefore, I am bequeathing Sage Advice to you, Sam Jones, on one condition: you must keep it open. You may not sell the business or the building. If this doesn't suit you, I understand. It's a lot to take on and if it's too much for you, my lawyer, Colin, has directions for Plan B.

You don't have the knowledge or experience to produce herbal remedies, but you're making a good attempt to learn. I hope you'll keep Annabelle on to assist you. She's a smart girl and her knowledge almost surpasses mine. What you do have is some business sense and you've become quite the asset to the displays of our goods. Hiring you was one of the best things I've done for the store in a long time.

I have thought long and hard about leaving the store to Annabelle, but it would be a mistake. She's excellent at mixing remedies but doesn't have a lick of business knowledge. She's an artist in her craft, not a businesswoman. She'd have to close the doors in less than a year.

The man who delivered this letter is a dear old friend. He can help you with everything from inventory to taxes as he's my lawyer and accountant.

I hope you'll decide to take care of my store, Samantha. And think about keeping Annabelle on. You two would make a wonderful team.

With love,

Bonnie

I SET down the paper and stared at it a long time, my heart galloping faster than a herd of wild horses.

Me? Owning Sage Advice?

As I glanced around the store, my emotions swirled. What had Bonnie been thinking? I'd only been around a few months. Her belief in me brought tears to my eyes. What did I know about running the business? Taxes? Permits? At least she'd pointed me in the direction of where to get help—Mr. Colin Breckshire III.

But then fear gripped my chest and I shut my eyes. Obviously, Bonnie had never planned on being murdered.

Now, out of everyone in town, I had become the one who had the most to gain from her death. And since I was the owner of the store she bequeathed me, it would make me the number one suspect.

CHAPTER 8

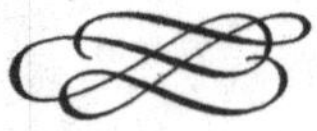

As soon as Annabelle returned, I left, stating I had an appointment I'd forgotten about. Thankfully, she didn't question me.

As I walked down Comfort Road, the main drag in town, tears stung my eyes. My first instinct upon receiving the letter was to run. To get into my car and leave the area, never to be heard from again. The only problem with that idea was my car was currently in the shop and Heywood was too small to support a rental car company. Besides, I'd somewhat adopted Catnip. I couldn't abandon him.

And the store. The store was an important fixture in the area for all the reasons Bonnie had listed.

When I passed Knit Wit, the knitting shop, I noted a group of women sitting in a circle, their hands busy with their projects, laughing and enjoying their time together. Cup of Go, the coffee shop, was also packed with people laughing and talking. Heywood was a community of true, authentic people… the exact opposite of the community I'd been a part of in Hollywood. And I wanted so badly to belong, to be one of them, to live a quiet, unassuming life—but here I was, smack in the middle of another murder investigation.

The cops would discover the store and building belonged to me, free and clear, since Bonnie had paid off her mortgage. If that wasn't motive, I didn't know what it was. Not to mention that I lived in said building, which gave me ample opportunity to convince Bonnie to accompany me down the Riverwalk, assuming that was where she was killed. I couldn't imagine anyone sticking a knife in her chest, dragging her down to the river, and dumping the body without being seen.

I should go to the police with the letter. Then it wouldn't seem as if I was hiding anything. I could explain it was just delivered today, and Colin Breckshire III could verify that.

However, they could argue that Bonnie had confided her plans to me about the store, and I killed her to hurry along the process. Most likely, they'd unravel my past, discover who I really was, and see this wasn't my first involvement in a murder.

And then what? I'd be the center of attention, which was exactly what I didn't want.

When I reached the end of the storefronts, I glanced over my shoulder at the little town I'd grown to love. Up ahead lay the highway which would take me out of the area, up by where I'd almost killed the deer. I could hitchhike out of town, but I quickly shut down that idea. It was dangerous and dumb.

What now?

I wanted to stay in Heywood. I loved it. Although I still hadn't come to terms with my past, I felt I could move forward by living here. And now, if I accepted, I'd have the weight of responsibility as the new owner of Sage Advice.

Turning to my left, I walked down the path leading to the Riverwalk. A gaggle of geese sat on a patch of lawn, eyeing me warily. Based on experience, I knew that if I offered them something to eat, they'd greet me. If not, they'd simply glare at me until I was out of sight.

I wrapped my sweater tighter around me. Fall was descending and the changing colors on the trees along the river never failed to take my breath away. I'd never seen such beautiful hues in Los Angeles. Yellows, oranges, and reds decorated the shore on the other side of the rushing water to my right. To my left, the restaurants, intermingled with the shops, still had people eating outside on the decks. I imagined in another couple of months, indoor dining would be a must due to cold weather and snow.

So, what was I going to do? Be chased out of town again for a crime I didn't commit to protect my identity, or stay and fight for the life I desperately wanted?

What would Cassie do?

She wouldn't run, that's for sure. In fact, she'd set out to find the killer… if she hadn't done it herself. If that was the case, she'd frame one of her enemies.

"That's what you need to do," I whispered to myself. "You need to find the murderer before they come looking to pin it on you."

With my rumination and pep talk now complete, I decided to pull together a plan. The four suspects I knew of so far, not including myself, were Bonnie's daughter, Catherine, Doctor Butte,

Annabelle, and Doug, the homeless guy. I needed to speak to all of them.

I didn't have much time to do anything else. Annabelle would wonder where I am, so I needed to head back that way, which would take me right past the bridge where Doug lived. Hopefully, I'd be able to find him and spend a few minutes talking with him about the killing. I'd seen him just before I found Bonnie so he had the opportunity to murder her. I just didn't know what his motive would be.

Sometimes, he disappeared from under the bridge, leaving all his belongings there unattended. I was never sure where he went, but I'd never bothered to ask, either.

As I hurried back toward the store and Doug's bridge, I smiled at the people passing by. Friends, lovers, moms with their kids, tourists… with each step, I became more convinced than ever that this was my community and I wouldn't give it up. Sticking my nose in a murder investigation was dangerous business, but I had to do it to protect myself from my past being revealed and to stay out of prison. The thought of Barry from the *Heywood Sentinel* writing a piece about my dead husband, the fraud, and the fire turned my stomach.

Passing the part where I found Bonnie's body proved difficult. I attempted to keep my stare averted from the bushes. It didn't work. I stopped and studied the area, her pink hat almost still visible to me in the heavy thicket, despite it having been removed days ago. Would I ever be able to erase the horrible images from my mind? Or at least learn to live with it?

When I killed someone on the soap opera, the blood and gore was always tame—daytime television demanded it. Bonnie hadn't been bloody either, the water washing away almost all indications of real life. I'd stepped over many bodies on *As the Years Turn*, but none of them could prepare me for my real-life experience with a murder victim. I had to find the killer not only for myself, but for Bonnie as well.

Resolved, I hurried to my destination. Hopefully, Doug could shine some light on the killing for me.

"Doug?" I called, approaching the bridge. "Are you around?"

I squinted in the afternoon sun into the shadows of the cave. His pile of belongings came into view, and finally, I spotted him sitting up against the wall. Hopefully, he wasn't high and we could have a coherent conversation.

"Doug?"

He glanced up and smiled through his thick beard. "Sam! Come over. I was just reading *Sapiens* by Yuval Noah Harari. Have you read it?"

I chuckled as I took a seat across from him. "No, that's bit above my bandwidth."

"Nah. You're a smart lady. It's a fascinating read on what it means to be human. I highly recommend it. I'll let you know when I'm done with it and return it to the library. You can check it out. Hey! We could have a little book club and discuss it!"

Doug represented the largest dichotomy of life to me. How could a man with such obvious intelligence live under a bridge and shoot himself up with heroin?

"Like I said, I think that book may be a little too smart for me." As my eyes adjusted, I noted that his seemed clear. This was the second time I'd seen him sober and I smiled. Could Doug be on his way to being totally clean?

"What can I do for you?" he asked, setting his book down on the ground next to him.

"Did you hear about Bonnie?" Our voices echoed off the cement walls, making our conversation seem louder than it was.

"I did. The news made me very sad. To think

that someone would do such a horrible thing to that woman... and right out in the open! I'm keeping a watchful eye now on everyone. I don't want someone knifing me in my sleep."

You and me both. "Do you remember when I saw you on the Riverwalk? The day she was killed?"

He tilted his head and furrowed his brow. "Was that the same day?"

"Yes, I'm certain of it. I was the one who found her body, so I have the day ingrained in my memories."

"You found her?" he asked, his eyes wide.

"I did. I was wondering if you saw anyone up that way when our paths crossed as you were walking toward the bridge."

He shook his head. "Not that I recall."

The problem speaking with Doug was that he freely admitted his memory wasn't the best and one day ran into another. He could've seen three people that day, but he may think it was a different one. It was beyond frustrating.

"Have the police been here to speak to you about it?"

"Yes."

"And what did you tell them?"

"I told them I saw you on the Riverwalk."

His words were like a punch to my gut. So not only did I have a motive in the police's eyes once they found out I was the heir to Bonnie's store, I was also present just after the killing. Even though I'd found the body, they could still look at me as a suspect. However, I'd also given his name to the police when they'd questioned me, so Doug and I were now even in my mind and I held no guilt for mentioning him. With a groan, I placed my head in my hands.

"What? What's wrong?"

I didn't reply.

"Oh. I see. You found the body. And me seeing you in that area beforehand... you think the police are going to think you did it."

I nodded.

"But you don't have any reason to kill Bonnie, do you?"

None, except for the fact I just inherited the store. I met his gaze again and tucked a lock of hair behind my ear. "No, I don't have a reason. She gave me a job and a place to live. Why would I want to kill her?"

Because now it all belongs to you.

"Who do you think did it?" he asked.

As I stared at the malnourished man with the long beard, his body odor wafting toward me like smoke, I couldn't help but wonder if he was responsible once again. First, he'd been in the general whereabouts. Second, he was a drug addict. Maybe it had been a robbery, or perhaps he hallucinated Bonnie being something she wasn't, and he felt he needed to destroy it in his stupor. And then he had the drugs to fall back on, if he said he didn't remember anything.

But this was also the homeless guy who'd picked up my wallet, which I'd dropped while jogging, and chased me down to return it. Did that sound like a murderer?

The drugs, though. Drugs made people do terrible things. They ruined the lives of not only the user, but those around them.

"Are you sure you don't remember seeing anyone else in that area?" I asked.

He shook his head as my phone began to ring. I pulled it out to see Annabelle trying to reach me. According to my watch, I'd been gone about an hour. I had to get back.

"I'd like to write down my number for you," I said, digging through my purse for a pen and an old grocery store receipt. I scribbled down my number and handed it to him. "If you think of anything else, will you call me? Anything you think could be helpful in finding out who killed Bonnie?"

"I don't own a phone, Sam," he said. "But I can use the one at the library. Besides, isn't finding the killer a job for the police?"

"Of course it is," I said, standing. "I'm just trying to figure out what happened that morning for my own peace of mind. Finding her body has had me very upset."

"I understand." He took the paper from me and placed it in the breast pocket of his shirt. "I'll give it a good think and call you."

As my phone shrilled in my pocket again, I broke out into a jog. "What's up, Annabelle?"

"Doctor Butte is here," she hissed. "Get back here *now!*"

CHAPTER 9

I HEARD the man yelling before walking into the store through the back door. Annabelle had done a heck of a job with the repair. The door open and shut with ease and didn't look half bad. With my lack of skills, I would've nailed it closed and dealt with it at another time. Or, in my former life, hired someone to fix it. Now, I'd have to subject myself to YouTube videos to figure out things like that. With my years of non-experience, I'd probably end up maimed from trying to use the nail gun.

Taking a deep breath, I marched through the back room into the store. Annabelle sat behind the counter, her shoulders hunched as if she were afraid she was going to be struck by the ranting lunatic in front of her.

"This store should be closed!" he yelled, his face the color of an apple. "The owner's dead! You don't have a business license in your name to operate!"

I gripped Annabelle's shoulder and gave her a squeeze. "Is there any reason for you to be yelling at her like this?" I asked. "Besides thinking you're important and you've decided the best tactic is to be a bully?"

"I'm trying to preserve the health and welfare of the citizens of our community!"

Shaking my head, I rounded the counter. "No, you aren't. You're trying to harass two women who have had their lives upended by the death of their friend, who also happened to be their boss."

"This has nothing to do with you two," he hissed. "I am a doctor. I am trying to protect the people of Heywood."

Crossing my arms over my chest, I narrowed my gaze on him. "Where were you the day Bonnie was killed?"

"Why do you ask?"

"Because someone killed her, and you sure seem intent on making sure she, or anything related to her, no longer exists."

Behind me, Annabelle muttered, "Don't mess with Cassie."

I almost cringed. She was right. How easily I slipped into my haughty character.

Butte blinked a couple of times, his brow furrowed in confusion. "Are... are you accusing me of killing her?"

"No. I'm asking where you were that day."

"It's none of your business."

I threw my head back and laughed, the sound deep and guttural, almost evil. My Cassie laugh. I recognized it as a distant memory. "You come in here making it your business what happens to us and to the store, yet, you won't tell me where you were the day she was killed? Because it's none of my business? This works two ways, doctor. If you stick your nose where it doesn't belong, expect the same to happen to you."

He fisted his hands at his sides, for I was getting under his skin. Good. Let him squirm and become uncomfortable. Perhaps he'd say something he'd end up regretting. A full confession would be lovely.

"I was in my office," he spat. For a second, I worried he'd strike me. Then, I almost wished he'd try. At least, that way, I'd get a restraining order and keep him out of the... *my* store.

A horrible idea occurred to me, and I went with it. "I think you're lying," I said, smiling.

He threw his arms up in the air. "Why? Why would I lie about something like that?"

"Because I know someone who saw you down by the Riverwalk," I replied, my voice low. "You were there, Doctor Butte, and the police will have the information soon, if they don't already."

The color drained from his face while his bluster seeped from him like air from a balloon. Was it because of guilt, or the fact he really hadn't done anything and the realization that he was being set up settled in? "I-I'm a doctor," he stammered. "I took an oath to do no harm. I'd never stab anyone."

"How did you know she was stabbed?" I asked. Even though I didn't read the *Heywood Sentinel*, the probability the mode of murder had been mentioned there was high. He could've found out by simply reading the news or overhearing it on the gossip grapevine.

"T-This is ridiculous," he stammered, then took a deep breath. "I won't be bullied and pushed around by two witchdoctors."

"And we won't be bullied or pushed around by a man who keeps his patients sick so they have to return to him for more and more drugs."

I'd gone too far. Oops.

"This won't be the last time you hear from me." He turned on his heel and strode out the door.

Standing in silence, I stared at him until he disappeared. *And cut. Scene end.*

"You really don't know someone who saw him down by the river that day, do you?" Annabelle asked.

I turned, somewhat surprised to find her there. "No."

"Why would you, like, tell him that?"

"Because I want him to leave us alone. Maybe if he thinks we know something, he'll give us some space."

"Perhaps," she murmured. "Or he could go to the police and tell them you're harassing him... spreading lies and stuff like that."

True. Perhaps I was the one who was going to end up with a restraining order against me.

"It's weird how you do that," Annabelle continued. "It's like you flip a switch inside you and suddenly, you're Cassie. Why do you do that?"

I sighed and busied myself rearranging a display table. "Just habit, I guess." In reality, it was so much more and boiled down to my own insecurities relating to my existence and identity. Once, I had a pretty good idea. But I was no longer the Emmy-nominated daytime television soap opera star, Samantha Rathbone. I was Sam Jones, faking my way through each day and hoping to stay hidden with nothing to define me. I hadn't rectified the two realities as I was still recovering from my life burning down both literally and figuratively. I probably needed a shrink. I'd had one back in Hollywood for a number of years, but I'd gone because seeing one was the "in" thing to do. Frankly, I hadn't gotten much out of the sessions. If I found one in the Heywood area, I'd probably make their head spin with the mess going on in my brain.

"I'm going to finish up some tinctures in the back, then take off," Annabelle said.

"Sounds good."

While Annabelle finished up her work, I cleaned the store once again in between helping customers. One wanted a tea to help her sleep. Another asked for something to ease her arthritis. After consulting with Annabelle, I steered her towards turmeric. Finally, it was time to close the store.

As I waved goodbye to Annabelle through the back door, my brain and heart felt as if they might explode. I needed to talk to someone, to share my secrets. My main confidant had always been Gerald, my dead husband. We had similar backgrounds, and even though our marriage wasn't driven by passion, he had been my best friend. His actions had cost me everything, but I still missed him. I'd never felt so alone.

When I finally pulled myself together, I walked slowly through the store, both terrified and excited. Mine. The store was mine. I imagined following Bonnie's plan—Annabelle and I teaming up together to run the place. We could do it, and we'd be successful. A perfect duo... if she hadn't killed Bonnie.

With a sigh, I headed upstairs and found Catnip waiting for me at the door. As he weaved in and out of my legs while I tried to walk into my small kitchen, he purred loudly and screamed for food. At least, he never left me guessing for what he wanted.

After feeding him, I poured a glass of wine and made a peanut butter sandwich, giggling to myself. Samantha Rathbone had never touched bread or pasta, and now, I indulged quite frequently. It felt good not feeling the pressure to always monitor my weight, and consequently, watch what I eat.

I turned on the television, and sank into the

couch. On the odd night when Gerald and I were home together watching a movie, he'd rub my feet while we shared one of his ridiculously expensive bottles of wine. Those were the times I missed the most, where we simply existed. No fancy dinners, no fundraisers, no phones... just us.

"And then he screwed it all up," I whispered as Catnip jumped onto my lap. My sadness dissipated a little as I stroked his back. "At least I have you, buddy."

The news was depressing, so I switched the channel to a rerun of *M.A.S.H.* I always found the show fascinating because it hit all the emotional markers. In one episode, I laughed until tears ran down my face; in the next, I was sobbing because it was so darn sad. They didn't make television shows like that any longer.

An hour later, I'd finished my dinner and debated whether I could go to bed so early and sleep until morning, or if I'd be pacing my apartment at three AM, cursing myself for not staying up later.

Catnip jumped from the couch and hurried to the door. For a long moment, he stared at the panel, then sat down, his tail swishing.

I muted the television, listening intently while watching him. Was someone in the building? And if so, how had they gotten in? I'd made sure to lock the doors before coming up. What the place really needed was an alarm system, but I'd never felt comfortable mentioning it to Bonnie while she was alive. Besides, this was Heywood, the small, idyllic town on the river, not Los Angeles or some other big city that was rampant with crime. However, we'd had one break-in, and based on the way the cat was acting, our second one may be occurring as I sat there. Now that I owned the building, I'd have to see how much it cost to have a security system installed.

I stood and tiptoed over to the door, pressing my ear against the panel. Nothing. Should I open the door? What if someone waited on the other side ready to pounce on me?

But for what? And who?

A serial killer? Someone who wanted me out of the picture?

A weapon. Why didn't I have a weapon?

I glanced around my apartment for something to use. Unfortunately, I didn't keep a baseball bat by the door. A chair? No. Too bulky. A knife? The idea of having someone's blood on me turned my stomach, so I didn't think I'd be able to use it. I vowed I'd head down to Locked and Loaded, the gun store, the first chance I got tomorrow and find some sort of protection to keep with me. Probably not a gun, but something.

Taking a deep breath, I slowly opened the door. Catnip raced back to the couch and curled up in a ball, watching me. "Coward," I whispered.

I stepped out into the hall and listened intently. Bonnie's door remained closed. I crept to her apartment, entered, and flipped on all the lights.

Nothing. I quickly checked each room, cursing under my breath. What was with Catnip? Why had he been acting so weird? Was he just strange, or had he actually heard something?

Just as I was about to turn off the lights and shut the door, something caught my eye on the taupe carpet. I bent down to pick up the red object.

A fingernail. A red, glue-on fingernail one could buy at any drugstore. It didn't belong to Bonnie. I couldn't recall ever seeing her with makeup on, let alone fake fingernails. It wasn't mine. I'd given up the makeup, nails, and blowouts when I left Hollywood.

Was it here when the police had searched the apartment and I hadn't seen it? Or had someone been at Bonnie's more recently?

I slid it into my pocket. Possibly a great clue. If

I found the owner of the nail, I'd maybe solve at least one of the mysteries: who had attacked me in Bonnie's apartment, and if the crime was related to Bonnie's murder, I'd also be able to discover who killed her.

CHAPTER 10

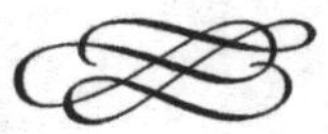

THE NEXT MORNING, I called Colin Breckshire and told him I would take Bonnie's offer and keep the store open. Then, I went for a jog. I found Doug passed out under his bridge, a needle at his side. After checking him for a pulse, I grabbed the dangerous object from the walkway and tucked it under the mat he laid upon, then covered him with one of his blankets while turning him so he didn't choke if he were to vomit. Drug addiction was a nasty thing.

"Doug?" I said loudly as I nudged his shoulder with the toe of my shoe. "Are you okay?"

He didn't move, but at least he was breathing. I stared at him for a long moment, wondering if he could've been out if his mind on something else besides heroin while killing Bonnie and not even have known he had. My interactions with drug addicts of Doug's level had been zero up until I moved to Heywood. In Hollywood, I had my status and wealth protecting me from this side of life. How the mighty had fallen.

I continued on my run, past the place I'd found Bonnie, all the way down to the end of the Riverwalk where the geese liked to hang out. As I breathlessly climbed the pathway to the main drag, Comfort Road, I promised myself I'd go running more often. My plan had been to jog back to the store, but I simply couldn't. Perhaps twenty years ago, or even ten years, but not today. Not at fifty-four. Instead, I'd take a nice stroll and call it good.

When I arrived at Locked and Loaded, I noted they were open and had customers inside. I guessed hunters were early risers, or something to that effect.

When I pushed on the door to enter, the smell of oil assaulted me. I glanced around at all the guns lining the walls, the hunting vests and tactical gear, and I pivoted to exit. I was way out of my element.

"What are you doing here, Sam Jones?"

I turned to find Deputy Jordan Branson

smiling at me. Dressed as he was in jeans and white tee with a red flannel shirt over it, I assumed this was his day off. Probably the last person I wanted to see. Without his uniform, he reminded me a bit of George Clooney.

"Just leaving," I said, waving. "Wrong store. Have a great day."

"I've never seen anyone walk into a gun store by mistake."

With a shrug and smile, I replied, "There's a first time for everything."

"Are you in the market for a gun?" he asked. I hesitated for a second, giving him the opportunity to continue the conversation. "Believe it or not, I've had some experience with them. I could help you out if you'd like."

How strange. Coming from Los Angeles, it was odd to find someone who wasn't horrified at gun ownership... and even willing to help me! But living in a small town in Arizona, I suppose I should've expected this, especially from the police.

"Have you ever handled a firearm before?" he asked.

I shook my head. Not a real one. Plenty of props on the set, though. I wouldn't be sharing that detail.

"Come on. I'll show you your options. For you, I'd recommend something smaller."

Reluctantly, I followed him over to the counter. As he pointed to different weapons and gave me a running commentary on the pros and cons of each one, I simply stared at them. So, so many guns in one place!

"I'd also suggest a safety class for you," he said. "It's not mandatory in Arizona, but I think it's a good idea. Safety is critical when handling firearms."

As I perused the weapons, I found it odd he didn't question *why* I felt I needed a gun. Perhaps everyone carried one and I was the exception?

"You'll always want to treat every gun as if it was loaded," he continued. "That's rule number one of gun safety."

This was a horrible idea. I didn't want a gun, just something to carry that made me feel better when Catnip started acting like the boogeyman stood outside my apartment door.

Smiling, I turned to the deputy. "A gun isn't for me. I was actually looking for some mace or something similar."

"Well, then I'll shut up and quit blathering on about gun safety," he said, chuckling.

"So, I'll just order some online. Thank you for your time."

"They have mace here." He pointed toward the far-right wall. I glanced behind me. Even mace came in many different sizes and shapes. "It's always best to shop local instead of those big online retailers. I'll show you the best kind."

Another small-town belief that I found comforting—supporting our local businesses. I followed him over and he pulled off a tube in a neon pink casing. It would've matched some of Annabelle's outfits.

"This is good because you can comfortably keep the mace in a pocket. The release is easy and quick and it sprays up to fifteen feet."

I liked that I didn't have to be really close to someone for it to be effective. And, I wouldn't kill anyone. Bonus points for the mace.

"Once you spray, you run like heck," he continued. "The chemicals incapacitate them for a short amount of time, but enough for you to escape."

"That sounds like what I need. Thank you, Deputy."

With a wide smile, he said, "You can call me Jordan."

Yeah, not going to happen. "Thank you."

I stepped over to wait in line to pay.

"Can I take you to get a cup of coffee?" he asked.

My head snapped to the side so quickly, I wouldn't be a bit surprised if I needed some ibuprofen later. "Excuse me?"

"Coffee. There's a coffee shop next door. Do you want to grab a cup?"

My first reaction was a hard pass, but something held me back from shutting down the idea.

He leaned in and whispered, "It's not a date."

I gasped and stepped away. "I-I never thought it was!" My word, this man was flustering me.

"So, will you go?"

While paying for my mace, I tried to think of the last time I'd sat down with someone for a cup of coffee. Even in Hollywood I'd had trouble nailing down my so-called friends. Everyone had been so busy, and most didn't want the extra calories a latte offered.

Cup of Go had the most beautiful views of the river. But, I'd yet to sit down in one of Heywood's restaurants and enjoy my surroundings simply because I'd never dined alone in public. The idea had always seemed so pathetic to me, so lonely. I *wanted* to join Deputy Branson, but I didn't know if it was the smartest, safest move. On the other hand, maybe I could squeeze a little information out of him.

"Sure," I said before I could overthink my decision. "As long as it's not a date."

The huge smile he gave me indicated he was pleased with my answer.

We strolled next door to the bustling shop and waited in line. I noted very few tables available, and none of them by the window overlooking the river, which was where I wanted to sit. When one couple stood, leaving one of those precious tables empty, I turned to Jordan. "Could you please order me an Americano with heavy cream? I'm going to grab that table over there."

His gaze followed me. "Good idea. Want a muffin or a scone?"

"Blueberry muffin," I called over my shoulder as I hurried to claim our chairs.

The view took my breath away. The River-walk, the river and the thick, dense forest on the other side made me feel as if I were sitting on the set of a Hallmark movie. Probably a Christmas film. All the elements were there: the wronged woman with the secret past who left the big city to start over in the small town... the dashing, good-natured cop... the beautiful setting. All that was needed was a whirlwind romance and the film would be complete. Except for the murder. I couldn't recall a Hallmark Christmas movie theme revolving around a killing. And there wouldn't be any romance. Instead, it would be a boring film with no plot, just a pretty setting.

"Here you go," Jordan said, setting down my cup and muffin in front of me. I took a sip as he settled in the chair across from me. "So, what brought you to Locked and Loaded that early in the morning?"

Choosing my words carefully, I answered, "I was out for a run and saw they were open. Now that I'm living alone in the building and we've had one break-in, I'm finding myself a little nervous."

He furrowed his brow in worry. "Have you had any other problems?"

I wasn't quite sure how to answer. Yes, Catnip had been acting strange the prior evening, and I'd found that fingernail in Bonnie's place, but nothing indicated there had been a break-in. All the doors had been locked. If there was someone in the building, it had to be Annabelle. She was the only one I knew who had a key. Unless someone else did and I wasn't aware of it.

"Not exactly," I hedged. "It's just a big place and I'm a little squirrely living there alone."

He laughed as he ripped apart his chocolate muffin. "Have you lived alone before?"

I shook my head. "Not recently." The direction of this conversation had to change. We were dancing dangerously close to him questioning who I was living with and where. "How is the investigation going, by the way?"

"Which one? The murder investigation or the breaking and entering into Sage Advice?"

I shrugged. "Either? Both?"

"Well, the official response is I'm not allowed to comment on ongoing investigations."

"And the unofficial response?"

"We're still looking at suspects."

"That doesn't sound much different from the official response," I said, smiling. "In fact, they're quite similar."

"Hey, at least I commented," he said, chuckling. "But to answer your question, we're nowhere near figuring out either case."

"I guess you don't consider me a suspect if you're sitting here having coffee with me," I ventured.

"Officially, no comment." His voice lowered. "Unofficially, I personally don't think you had anything to do with Bonnie's murder."

I nodded, relief flooding through me.

"But I do think you're hiding something. What that is, I'm not quite sure of."

"Why do you think that?"

"You're one of the most closed off people I've ever met. You smile when you're supposed to, but I feel like you're acting. Like I'm not seeing the real Sam Jones."

I fought to keep my features as neutral as possible. Was I that transparent? Or was he that good of a cop? And really, had I figured out who the real Sam Jones was?

"So, why don't you tell me one of your well-kept secrets?"

Suddenly, the store seemed quite warm, and it wasn't a hot flash. The conversation was making me quite uncomfortable.

But at the same time, something inside me did want to confide in him. I didn't have to tell him my past, but I could share my other secret. He'd already agreed I had nothing to do with Bonnie's murder, and it seemed better if he found out about the will directly from me. Otherwise, I looked like I had something to hide.

"A lawyer visited me yesterday," I said. "Bonnie's lawyer."

"Oh? And what did he have to say?"

"Bonnie left Sage Advice to me."

He didn't bother to hide his shock. "What?!"

I glanced around to see if he'd drawn attention. A couple people turned toward us, but most kept their attention on their own tables. "She also left me a letter," I said, my voice quiet. Hopefully, he'd take the hint and lower his.

He leaned forward, his tone quieter. "Do you have it with you? What does it say?"

"No, it's at home. The letter says she and her daughter, Catherine, are estranged, and she doesn't want her to have the store."

Jordan let out a low whistle and sat back in his chair. "Catherine isn't going to like that."

"I'm sure she won't." After finishing off the rest of my blueberry muffin, I asked, "Is she still in town?"

"From what I understand, yes. She's trying to track down her mother's will. It sounds like you're way ahead of her on that one, though."

Perhaps that's what had happened last night—Catherine had been searching Bonnie's apartment for the will.

"I have the lawyer's number at home. Should I pass it on to you so you can give it to her?"

"Sure. If you could text it to me, that would be great." He pulled out his phone, and seconds later, mine shrilled. "I kept your number for investigation purposes."

I picked up the device and assigned a name to the number, unsure how I felt about him having my contact details in his phone. Perhaps it was normal for an investigator to keep them on his personal device? Or perhaps he carried a department issued phone? "Do you still think I'm innocent?"

He nodded. "I do, even if this piece of news gives you motive."

"That's why I was afraid to tell you about it." I took a long sip of my coffee. "I came to Heywood to have a quiet life. I don't want any trouble."

"I get it," he replied. "That's why I'm here as well."

Once again, I wondered what circumstances had led him to Heywood, but that would open up a conversation I didn't want to have.

For the next hour, we chatted about restaurants and hiking trails in the area, none of which I'd experienced.

"Maybe someday I'll take you on a hike and we'll go out to dinner," Jordan said, grinning. "But of course, it won't be a date."

I smiled, having thoroughly enjoyed my time with him, when my bitterness subsided for a short while. "I should get going. And yes, I'd like that… as long as it isn't a date."

After I walked out of Cup of Go and turned down the street to head towards Sage Advice, I studied my unread messages. Annabelle had texted me to let me know she'd be a little late, but that was it. I glanced up then to see Bonnie's daughter, Catherine, up ahead, entering a store, so I hurried to catch up to her, unsure what I was going to say.

I stopped dead in my tracks as she entered one of the buildings. Last night I'd found a red nail in Bonnie's apartment. And now, her daughter was at a nail salon.

CHAPTER 11

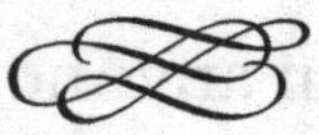

FOR THE REST of the day, I studied people's fingernails. Just because I'd seen Catherine walk into the nail salon didn't necessarily mean she had been the one in Bonnie's apartment. I was trying to give her the benefit of the doubt.

Annabelle wore blue, sparkly paint, which looked fresh to my trained eye, but I couldn't quite decipher if they were real or fake since they were trimmed short. Trying to remember what she wore yesterday was futile, but I couldn't rule out that it had been red and she'd lost one searching Bonnie's apartment.

"Annabelle, do you know who else may have a key to this place?"

She shook her head. "For a long time, it was

just me and Bonnie, then you came along. I've never seen her give one to anyone else."

So, if the building had been locked and Annabelle was the only one with a key, I had to assume she was in Bonnie's apartment the prior night… if there'd been anyone in there at all, which still hadn't been determined. But then there was the fact the cops had missed the nail—as had I—and that someone had pushed me down a few nights ago.

"I think we should change the locks," I said. If we did, and I had issues with someone creeping around after hours again, I knew for sure it would be Annabelle.

"Do you think that's a good idea? I mean, like, we don't even know who owns the building at this point."

"True," I lied. "But I know I'd feel safer here at night with them changed. Besides, when the owner is revealed, we can hand over the keys. They'll never even know the locks were recently changed."

"Do you want me to call the guy down at Hammer and Nail Hardware? I think his name's Chris."

"That would be great, thank you."

"Oh, and also, someone needs to take these

blends out to the Tupper farm." She grabbed a paper sack from the counter and held it up.

Tupper… Tupper… why did I know that name?

"I'll take it," I said. "It's better for you to stay here in case anyone has questions I'm not able to answer."

"Yuppers. Do you know where you're going?"

I shook my head.

"Charlie and Doreen Tupper live out on Route 9. Let me draw you a map. You probably won't get reception out there to use Google."

The name finally rang a bell. Charlie Tupper had been the one to stop and help me after I hit the deer. I walked over and looked in the bag. "That's a lot of stuff."

"Doreen has cancer," she said. "It's terminal. She's not receiving any further traditional treatment. Basically, she's waiting to die. But, I do have to say, she's getting along really well. Sometimes I wonder if she's been misdiagnosed. She's like the energizer bunny."

"Oh, that's awful." Charlie hadn't mentioned it when we'd met, but it wasn't really news to be shared with strangers.

"She was getting treatment in Sedona before

she decided to call it quits," Annabelle continued. "Charlie says Butte's a witchdoctor."

Interesting. That term seemed to be thrown around a lot in Heywood. "Seems like he's not the only one who feels that way."

"Right? If it walks like a duck and quacks like a duck, then it's a witchdoctor."

"Not a duck?"

We both snickered at our bad jokes.

"Would you mind if I took your car for the delivery?" I asked. Mine's still in the shop."

"You should call and see what's the deal with that. It shouldn't take that long to tell you what it's going to cost to fix it. And yes, you can take my car. Just don't run into any deer."

"Could you also call the Tuppers and let them know I'm on my way?"

"Yes ma'am. Now, get out of here so I can finish filling these capsules. The customer will be by later today."

After she threw me her keys, I grabbed the paper bag and strolled out the front door, my mood light for the first time in ages.

As I drove out of town—in the opposite direction from where I'd almost hit the deer—I marveled at the beauty of the area. Long swaths of farmland stretched to the mountains. Some grew flowers, others food. I tried to reason why I hadn't ventured out this way, and I realized I really hadn't ventured at all. My apartment had become my sanctuary of safety from my past as I tried to heal myself. Today had proven that I needed to get out more, to try to socialize and see the world around me.

I held the map and directions Annabelle had written in one hand as my gaze bounced from it to the road in front of me.

Turn right at the second oak tree, not the first. The first is the Wilbur farm.

Chuckling, I did as instructed, appreciating the simplicity.

I found Charlie's farm about a mile down the dirt road, his house nestled in the middle of a swath of trees. A barn and corral complete with horses stood to the left of the yellow home with the wraparound porch, and beyond that, all I could see were crops for miles.

"Wow," I whispered as I parked and exited the car. It was beautiful. A perfect setting for an old western movie where the husband has been killed because someone wants his land and it's up to his wife to fight to keep it. I could practically see the woman, her skirts swirling around her ankles as she burst out onto the porch, shotgun in hand, ready to defend what was hers.

I stood for a moment, taking it all in when movement by the barn caught my eye. Charlie strode out and waved. "Hey, Sam!" he yelled as he approached. "Welcome to the farm!" A little white and brown goat trotted behind him.

I met Charlie halfway and handed him the bag. "This is lovely."

He glanced around and nodded. "Yep. Like I told you, it's been in my family for a few generations. Costs a pretty penny to run it, though. My son is going to be taking it over after I'm gone or decide to hang up my overalls… whichever comes first. That boy's got a brain bigger than four of mine put together."

The little goat bayed and began chewing on my shoelaces. "That's Barney," he said, nudging him with his foot. "He'll eat anything."

Barney was not to be deterred and returned immediately to my laces.

"Can I give you a tour of the place?" Charlie asked.

I glanced around and nodded. "I'd like that."

Barney scampered next to me as I followed Charlie toward the barn. A horse came over to greet us as Charlie opened the gate to the corral.

"That's Trinity. She's as sweet as they come, so if you're afraid of horses, there's nothing to worry about."

Growing up in Oakland and spending my life in Hollywood, I didn't get around too many animals except for the odd dog or cat at a friend's home. Most of my work had been on *As the Years Turn* and a few Hallmark movies, and horses had never been part of the plot. Reaching out, I allowed the beast to sniff my hand, then pet her long snout. In return, she sniffed my jacket pockets.

"She'll steal whatever's in there. Keys, tissues, money… that's her game. I'd recommend zipping up all pockets if you can."

Since I didn't have any zippers, I shoved my hands in them to block the burglar and followed Charlie the rest of the way to the barn. There, I found more goats, a few chickens and the miniature cows he'd mentioned when I'd first met him. I leaned down and pet a white one that stared up at me with big brown eyes, standing no more than three feet tall. I'd never seen anything sweeter.

"I told you they were cute, didn't I?"

"Yes. Yes, you did," I said, chuckling. Barney tried to stand between me and the cow, vocally letting me know he was the one I should be petting.

"Barney there likes all the attention on him, if you didn't notice," Charlie said. "He's spoiled rotten. That cow's name is Snowflake. She likes to play chase with the dog, Daisy."

"Where is Daisy?" I remembered the Golden Retriever well from when Charlie had driven me home after my accident.

"She's inside with Doreen."

I stood upright. "How's she feeling?"

"Pretty good. Glad to have her around as long as possible. She's not taking any more treatment."

I nodded, not sure what to say. Everything that came to mind seemed so insincere.

"The herbs from Sage Advice help a lot, so thanks for delivering them. The ginger really eases her nausea."

"Of course. I'm glad I could bring them out."

"Have you met Doreen?"

I shook my head, glancing around the barn again. In a very short period of time, I'd fallen in love with the Tupper farm.

"Come on inside, Sam. I told her about my gallant rescue on the highway. She'll want to meet you."

With a snicker, I followed him into the house.

A warm living room decorated in taupe and sea moss green greeted me. Based on the cracks, the overstuffed brown couch had seen many years of use. Picture frames stood on the mantel above the fireplace.

"Let me grab her," Charlie said, striding into what I assumed would be the kitchen. "Doreen!"

Daisy bounded around the corner, tail wagging, and sniffed my feet.

"Well, hello there," I said softly as I stroked her head. "Do you remember me?"

After a moment, Daisy lost interest in me and trotted off down the hall. I studied the photos on the mantel carefully and assumed most were of their children and grandchildren.

One photo in particular caught my eye and I picked up the frame to examine it closer. Who was this woman? I felt I knew her, or at least I'd seen her. The realization hit me like a ton of bricks.

Catherine. Bonnie's daughter. The picture had been taken years ago, but there was no doubt it was her.

What in the world was a picture of Catherine doing in Charlie's house?

I set it down as the couple entered. A woman, also in her seventies, greeted me with a warm smile as she shook my hand. "It's so lovely to meet you," she said. "I'm Doreen. I can't thank you enough for bringing my herbs."

For someone with terminal cancer, she was quite spry and looked very healthy despite the bright pink and green scarf wrapped around her bald head, and being rail thin. Her blue eyes twinkled as she smiled.

"My pleasure. You have a beautiful place here."

"Oh, yes. We love it. Been in Charlie's family for generations. I just made some lemonade. Would you care to join us for a glass out on the porch?"

"I would love to, but I should really be getting back to the store," I said, meaning every word. I could stay on this farm for the rest of my life.

"We heard about Bonnie," Doreen said, shaking her head. "Such a shame. Have you been in touch with her daughter, Catherine, at all?"

I glanced over at the photo. "Only briefly, but I noticed you had a picture of her."

Charlie stared wistfully at the frame. Were his eyes tearing up? "She's my daughter. Bonnie and I had a fling before I married Doreen, and Catherine was the result."

Well. Blow me over with a gust of wind. I never saw that one coming.

"She's not a nice person," Doreen said. "We haven't spoken to her in years, but we assumed she'd come sniffing around once she heard about Bonnie's death. We keep the picture to remind ourselves that she always hasn't been awful."

"Yes," I replied. "She's been around."

"She'll want the store and everything that's Bonnie's," Doreen said, crossing her arms over her chest. "She'll sell it all."

Charlie nodded. "Not sure how she became so greedy."

"She'd sell her soul for a pair of Gucci shoes," Doreen muttered.

There wasn't any animosity between the couple regarding Charlie's out of wedlock daughter, which I found refreshing. However, they seemed to be bonded in their utter dislike of the woman.

"I'm surprised she hasn't shown her face around here," Charlie said. "Last time we saw her, she tried to get me to sign documents giving everything to her. Told me I wasn't in my right mind and she thought I had dementia."

He seemed quite sharp to me. "When was that?" I asked.

"Years ago. Haven't seen or heard from her since."

"Catherine wanted the farm for herself," Doreen said, shaking her head. "My guess is that she wanted to sell it to a developer or something, because she doesn't have any farming blood in her." She grimaced in disgust. "We've got everything locked down tight, though. It all goes to our kids, with her getting a small stipend. Hopefully, she'll let matters lie."

"I doubt it," Charlie muttered. "But I won't have a sword in that fight."

"I'm sorry for the trouble she's caused you," I said.

"We are too," Charlie sighed. "Sometimes you have kids and they're a mirror of your soul. That's my son. He's a good boy with values and a moral compass. Other times, you barely recognize them as one of your own. That's Catherine."

"Such a shame," Doreen said. "Such a waste."

I stayed a few more minutes then took my leave. After saying our goodbyes, I drove the dirt road out to the main highway. Turning left, I settled in for my ride back to Heywood proper.

Next time Doreen needed her herbs, I was going to allot more time at the farm so I could play with the little cows and goats. Could a mini cow live in my apartment with Catnip? Probably not. And training a cow to use the toilet was a whole other ball of wax I didn't have time for, if it could even be done.

What a perfect day, though. Coffee with someone who I could see becoming a friend, as long as I was careful with my identity. Meeting mini cows, having my shoe chewed on by the cutest little goat... for the first time in a long time, I felt joyful. So much so, it brought tears to my eyes.

That was until I pulled up in front of the store to find Sheriff Mallory Richards waiting for me.

As I STRODE into the store, I met the sheriff's gaze and tried to paste on a smile, yet, I couldn't help but think her visit wouldn't bring good news.

"There you are," she said, her gaze trailing over me from head to toe. "We've been trying to call."

"I was out of range. What can I do for you?"

"Can I speak to you outside?"

I glanced over her shoulder at Annabelle who shrugged, obviously having no idea what was happening. Today, she wore an off-the-shoulder neon-green shirt, jeans, and white legwarmers. Her blue eyeliner also seemed particularly thick while her long, crimped hair almost stood on end with volume.

But back to the thin, muscular woman in front of me wearing a gun. "Of course."

We stepped out to the front of the store and I realized we were in full view of everyone, which I didn't like. Passersby gaped at us, not bothering to hide their curiosity. "Can we go around the side of the building?" I asked.

"Why?"

"I'm a private person," I replied. "I prefer to keep my business to myself."

"Fine."

She followed me around to the small alleyway between Sage Advice and Knit Wit. "What can I do for you, Sheriff?"

"I want to see this magical letter that you claim to have."

My good mood deflated faster than a pin-pricked balloon and my anger and bitterness returned in full force. Jordan seemed to have gone from our coffee chat directly to his boss.

"It's inside," I lied. I actually had it stuffed in my bag. I wasn't letting it out of my sight. "Maybe you should talk to the lawyer who gave it to me. Colin Breckshire, the second or the third. I can't remember what he said. I have his number."

She narrowed her gaze. "Listen, Ms. Jones. When I ask you for something, you give it to me.

I am the sheriff of this town, not someone to be brushed off or toyed with."

I put on a polite smile and avoided mentioning the fourth amendment that protected me from people like her. "I'm not handing over personal property."

"You most certainly will. I'm investigating a murder and that letter is evidence. You're lucky I don't lock you up for obstruction."

Did she have the right to take the letter? A lawyer would know, but I didn't have one of those. Maybe I should call Colin. Could he be my lawyer as well as executor of Bonnie's estate? Or was that a conflict of interest?

Mallory sighed and shook her head. "We can do this the easy way, or we can do it the hard way."

"Can you explain the two to me?"

"Don't be a smart mouth," she hissed. "I'm seconds away from cuffing you and hauling you to jail."

"I think I'm within my rights to know my options," I replied, trying to keep the Cassie out of my voice, even though I'd like nothing more than to unload on her.

As her cheeks turned fiery red, she set her hands on her gun belt. "You either give me that letter now, or I take you to jail and I close down Sage Advice, do another full search of the building, and then a cavity search of you, just because I can."

I longed to slap the power out of the woman, but my more sensible side took over. If she hauled me off to jail, Barry from the *Sentinel* would do a piece on me. Chances were good my true identity would be revealed. Besides, a cavity search didn't sound like any fun whatsoever, and I had a feeling she wouldn't be gentle.

"Let me grab it for you," I said, turning and heading into the store. I knew my rights, and I also knew my good sheriff was violating them. But I also wanted to cause as little trouble as possible, and if that meant handing over property Mallory had no business requesting, then so be it.

She followed close behind.

Annabelle greeted me with a wide stare. I saw at least four thousand questions in her gaze, but both of us remained silent. As I circled the counter, the sheriff asked, "Where are you going?"

"To get you the letter. Please stay there. Our back room is full of bottles and powders. We can't have anything touched or moved."

She grumbled as I continued through the back room into a closet where we kept the printer, which also acted as a scanner. I laid the letter on the flatbed and waited for it to warm up. A moment later, a copy of the letter came out the other end. But which one did I give her? The copy or the original? Could a copy be declared insufficient in a court of law? I had to assume so. I shoved it back into my bag and slung it over my shoulder.

Taking a deep breath, I returned to the front of the store and handed Mallory the copy.

"Thank you," she muttered as she read it over. "Let's go back outside, Ms. Jones."

With a sigh, I followed her out the door and back around the corner.

She stared at me a for a long beat, then said, "I'm going to give you some advice. Don't leave town. If I come to the conclusion that you killed Bonnie and I can't find you around to arrest you, I'll hunt you down like a rabid dog. Have I made myself clear?"

How friendly and polite. Pursing my lips together, I nodded. Jordan had specifically said he didn't think of me as a suspect, but apparently, the top boss did. Once again, I learned the hard way I couldn't trust anyone. I wished I'd been a fly on the wall while he revealed the news to her. Had they laughed at how easily I'd been played?

That I'd fallen for his charm and smile? That I was a lonely woman, desperate for a friend, so I'd confided in a cop?

"Have a good day, Ms. Jones. I better see you around."

I returned to the store and tried to put on a happy face for Annabelle.

"What in the world is going on?" she asked.

"The sheriff needed something from me."

"What did you give her?"

"Some paperwork about the store," I replied, hoping she didn't question me any further.

"She seemed really angry."

"Agreed." I had to change the direction of this conversation. Annabelle would be asking questions I didn't want to answer. "Did you know the Tupper farm has miniature cows?"

As I shared my farm experience with her, her eyes danced with happiness. I wanted to trust Annabelle, but I couldn't. She could very well have thought that if Bonnie was dead, she'd get the store. And the fact she seemed to have given a lot of thought to future plans for Sage Advice again made me question if she could be the murderer.

"I wonder if Charlie would mind if I went out and saw the little darlings," she mused.

"Next time we need to deliver out there, we'll go together," I said, hoping that would be true.

"Bonnie always took Doreen's herbs out to her." Her smile faded. "She'd be gone for hours at a time. I sure miss her."

"Me, too."

"What about, like, a funeral?" Annabelle asked. "Who's putting that together? When is it?"

"I... I have no idea." I hadn't given it any thought, but perhaps the lawyer would know. "I can make some phone calls and find out."

"If you could, that would be great," she said. "Although, I wouldn't be the least bit surprised if Bonnie didn't want a fuss made about her."

"You're probably right," I said. "But I'll call anyway. If there's going to be one, I wouldn't want to miss it."

The day passed by quickly, customers filtering in and out. I listened in on a couple of Annabelle's consultations with those who came in with specific problems. With kindness and caring, she studied the teen boy with horrible acne and asked him questions as I and his mom looked on. What made it worse? Did anything make it better? What did he eat throughout the day? Sugar consumption? Did he drink caffeinated drinks? What did he use to wash his face? She listened intently while the mother listed off the other methods they'd tried to clear the acne. After spending at least forty-five minutes with him, Annabelle asked him to wait for a bit and hurried to the back room, returning moments later with a soap set she wanted him to try.

"You wash with this," she said, holding up the bar. "Then, I want you to take a cotton ball and gently rub this on your face. Actually, don't rub. Dab it." She pointed to a small, plastic bottle filled with liquid. "Drink at least eight glasses of water each day, and no sugar. Let's see if that diet change makes a difference. Then, in thirty days, I want you to come back so I can see your progress."

The kid groaned, claiming he loved ice cream, but Annabelle gently chided him, stating it was only for a month. "After that, if it doesn't make an improvement, you can eat it by the gallon if your mom gives the okay. If it does help clear your face, my guess is that you won't want any."

Annabelle's demeanor didn't really match up with a killer's but what did I know? I'd only played one on television. Yes, in real life, my boss had murdered my husband and I'd known him fairly well, but when I'd discovered he was responsible for Gerald's death, it hadn't surprised me all that much.

I couldn't get past the fact that Annabelle's whole life seemed to be invested in this business. She had plans for the store's future. But if she was the murderer, I'd be shocked. Her demeanor was too kind, too gentle.

"What did you give him?" I asked when the teen and his mom left the store.

"Chamomile soap and some witch hazel. I think we'll probably need to try something else, but hopefully it will at least calm the breakouts."

"You're really good with the customers," I said.

"Thank you," Annabelle replied, her smile wide. "That means a lot to me. I remember what it's like to be at the end of your rope and need help. It's not always easy to ask for it, especially for the teens."

As I went along with the rest of my day, a plan began to form. Obviously, the sheriff had me in her crosshairs. I was the one who had the most to gain from Bonnie's death. If I did nothing, I feared I'd end up in jail for a crime I didn't commit, as well as have my past all over the front-page news. I'd become fodder for late night jokes, and I could practically hear the gossip headlines:

You thought her husband was a thief? Samantha Rathbone steals lives!

Samantha Rathbone, living another life, arrested for murder!

We need to ask ourselves if Samantha Rathbone killed her husband, because she's killed an old woman!

And even if I was cleared for the murder, I'd still have the cloud of assumed guilt hanging over me. Maybe I should've gotten out of here when I had the chance, but there had to be a way for me to retain my anonymity as well as keep Sage Advice and my life in Heywood. I didn't want to run anymore.

The only way I could find to reach all my goals was to solve Bonnie's murder myself.

And I knew exactly what my next step would be.

CHAPTER 13

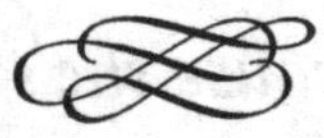

I WAITED UNTIL AFTER HOURS, then approached File It Away, the nail salon. Having walked by a few times, I'd never really paid much attention to the business since I never wanted to have my nails professionally done ever again. The sign on the door said closed, but a woman was inside, sweeping. I tapped on the glass. She shooed me away and turned her back to me. Not to be deterred, I knocked again.

She strode over to the door, showing her anger and irritation with a grimace. Long, blonde hair cascaded around her thin shoulders as she pushed her tortoiseshell glasses up her nose. Probably somewhere in her forties.

"We're closed!" she yelled, tapping the sign indicating as much.

"I know," I replied, smiling. "And I'm sorry to bother you. I just need to ask you a few questions. I won't take much of your time, I promise."

She flipped the lock on the door and opened it, motioning me inside. "Listen. My son just called and my dog is about to have puppies. I don't have time for a chat. I need to get this place cleaned up and go home. If you want to make an appointment, I open tomorrow at noon." She glanced down at my hands. "Yeah, you definitely need to come in."

While curling my fingers, my face heated. Yes, my nails were a mess, but I'd made a promise to myself when I left Hollywood to live a simpler life. I'd go without all the fakeness and let nature take its course. Perhaps I'd taken it too far with simply cutting and filing my nails, but I would stick to my plan.

"How about I help you clean up while we chat?" I asked.

She narrowed her gaze, then glanced over her shoulder and back at me. "Who are you?"

"I'm Sam Jones. I work at Sage Advice."

"Bonnie's store," she said, sighing. "Poor thing."

"Yes, we're all quite upset."

"I haven't seen you around."

"I'm new in town. Can I come in and help you sweep? Ask you a few questions?"

"I suppose so. I'd appreciate the help. I'm Gina Dunner, by the way."

"It's nice to meet you. Where would you like me to start?" Glancing around the store, I found the brown and blue interior inviting and calming.

She hurried over to some shelves and pulled out a spray bottle and a rag. "You can wipe down the bowls."

After taking the items, I dropped to my knees in front of one of the chairs and sprayed the taupe-colored bowl. Having spent thirty years in Hollywood being catered to, I'd rarely done manual labor. In fact, since landing in Heywood, I'd done more cleaning than I had in my entire adult life, and I found myself appreciating the simple tasks simply because I was accomplishing something completely normal.

"What did you want to talk to me about?" Gina asked.

"Early this morning, you had a woman in here named Catherine. I was wondering what color nail polish she had on."

Gina snorted and shook her head, resuming

her sweeping. "I don't remember the name of every customer."

"Catherine is Bonnie's daughter," I said, wiping the bowl and hoping to shake her memory.

"Oh! Her! Yeah, she was in here. She made sure everyone knew she was Bonnie's daughter… almost like she was fishing for sympathy."

"Did she get it?"

"Some. A lot of people weren't too fond of Bonnie. If you got on her bad side, she could be mean."

And there it was again. Bonnie had a bad side —one I'd never met.

"Can you give me an example?" I asked.

"Well, I've never personally had any bad dealings with Bonnie, but I've heard stories. When Knit Wit had to have the front of their building dug up for a water leak, Bonnie called the cops."

"Why?"

"Because the guy running the jackhammer started a half hour early, breaking the noise ordinances in town. She lived in the building and didn't like the sound."

Couldn't blame her, but calling the police seemed petty at best.

Gina continued. "This was a couple of years

ago, but she got into an argument with someone over a parking spot at the grocery store. Two days later, that person found a nail in their tire."

"And they think Bonnie put it there?"

"Or she laid it under the tire for them to run over," Gina said, shrugging. "No one could ever prove it though."

Interesting. The sweet, old woman I'd known had a bit of a passive-aggressive streak in her.

"Do you know Catherine?" I asked, changing the subject.

"No. I'd never seen her before. I remember her from earlier because she kept talking about Sage Advice and Bonnie."

I sat back on my heels. "What did she say?"

"Keep scrubbing," Gina said. "I need to be there for the birth."

Moving to the next bowl, I repeated my question as I sprayed it down.

"Just that she was going to own the building where Sage Advice is located, and she was thinking of all the things she wanted to do with it."

"What does that mean?" I asked.

"She was pretty adamant that she wouldn't be keeping the herb store, that she wanted to do something else with the building."

"Like what?"

"Yoga. She talked about gutting the inside and putting in a yoga studio. Said she'd always wanted to own her own business."

I finished up the third bowl and stood. "Did she say when she planned to take ownership of the building?"

"Apparently, she's meeting with the lawyer running the estate next week." She bent down and swept everything into the dustpan. "Why do you want to know all this?"

"Just curious," I said. Catherine was in for quite the surprise when she met with Colin Breckshire. "She's come around the store a lot lately, and she's not very nice."

"That I can agree with," Gina said, dumping the contents of the dustpan into the garbage. "She's got a hoity toity attitude about her. She wanted everyone to know that she lives in Paradise Valley, just outside of Phoenix, and she dropped famous people's names like candy. She's full of herself."

Paradise Valley was one of the most upper scale neighborhoods in the Phoenix area, and if one was to meet a celebrity, that would be the place to do it. Either Paradise Valley or Scottsdale. In my former life, I had friends who spent time in the valley and they always stayed in that area. My time in Phoenix had consisted of a night in a budget motel, as well as a couple of hours while I cashed out and closed my bank account before heading north.

"How long have you lived in Heywood?" I asked.

"My whole life," she said, sighing. "I should've gotten out when I had the chance."

I had no idea what that could possibly mean, but I didn't question it. "And you'd never seen or met Catherine before?"

Gina shrugged. "Not that I recall. Why?"

"I find it odd that she showed up in town right when her mother died and now, she's talking about how she's going to close Sage Advice and open a yoga studio."

"She may be full of herself, but she's not very smart. She hasn't read the town or done her research. There was a yoga studio here two years ago. They were in business for six months before they had to close their doors."

"Why?"

"There isn't the market for one," she replied. "Our population is too small and the farmers aren't interested in yoga. The tourists are here to eat, hike, and float down the river, not take a yoga class. Heck, I'm only open three days a week for a few hours each day. This salon's my side gig."

"Did you tell her any of that?"

Gina shook her head. "Nope. None of my business what people want to waste their money doing. Besides, I don't think she'd listen to me anyway. She didn't seem like the type who wanted to hear that she was making a mistake."

My assessment of Catherine matched Gina's, and I'd only met Bonnie's daughter for a few moments.

"What's your regular job?" I asked.

"I have quite a few, actually. I'm a writer, and also a dog rescuer. Most of my writing jobs come online. I submit articles for publication and do some ghostwriting. What I should do is just write my own darn books, but it's hard when you have dogs to take care of around the clock."

"How many dogs do you rescue a year?"

"It depends. The next couple of months are going to be tough with those pups being born. Should I put you down for one? Mama's a sweet, blonde lab."

"No thanks. I'm taking care of Bonnie's cat right now. I don't think throwing a puppy into the mix would be a good idea."

"That's too bad." She hurried over to a closet

and set the broom and dustpan inside. "And I need to get home to help my mama through the birth."

I nodded, desperate for information. Of course, I didn't want to keep her, but I had a couple of other questions. "What about Catherine's nails? What was the condition of them?"

Gina snapped her fingers and pointed at me. "I remember now. She had one missing, snapped off."

"What color?" I held my breath, waiting for the answer.

"Red. Blood red."

Finally, I was getting somewhere. Catherine most likely had been in Bonnie's apartment; I just didn't know when. Was it before the murder, or after? And had she been the one who'd pushed me to the floor?

"Are we done cleaning?" I asked, glancing around. "Is there something else you'd like me to do?"

Gina surveyed the store with a critical eye for a long moment. "Nope. I think we're good here. Thanks for your help. I hoped I answered your questions."

"You gave me a lot to think about. Thank you."

When we stepped outside, a cool breeze caused goosebumps on my skin.

"Winter's coming," Gina said, pulling the keys from her pocket and locking the door. "I hope it's a good one, too. We need the moisture."

"How much snow do we usually get?" I asked.

"It depends, but our average is about eighty-one inches a year."

"That's a lot of snow," I muttered. Having never lived in a snowy climate, I made a mental note to figure out what needed to be done to prepare. Sure, I'd spent some time in Aspen and in the Alps, but that had been for vacation. First off, I'd need a parka and some boots. Did I need to do something special to the Sage Advice building? Heck, if things got any worse for me, I may be spending my first snowy winter in prison. Another chill ran down my spine at the thought.

"Have a good evening, Sam," Gina said, turning and hurrying down the street in the opposite direction I was headed.

I slowly began my walk back to Sage Advice while thinking about the nail.

"Oh! Sam!"

I turned to find Gina jogging toward me. "What's that woman's name who works with you?

Who looks like she's stuck in the Pretty in Pink movie?"

"Annabelle?"

"Yes! Her! I can never remember her name. Even though we grew up in the same town, we didn't have much to do with each other. We ran in different crowds, I guess."

But you share the same lover. Gina had to be aware of that detail, didn't she?

"That's another thing about Catherine," she continued. "When she left, Annabelle was waiting for her out on the street. They talked for a few moments."

I gasped in surprise. "Did… were they arguing? Did they seem like they knew each other?"

"It was a short conversation, but it didn't seem contentious in any way. They definitely knew each other."

"Thanks, Gina. Good luck with the puppies."

The news hit me like a punch to the gut. If Gina was correct, Annabelle and Catherine could be in cahoots together. Annabelle had acted so innocent about Catherine, claiming she didn't know her. Liar. I was right to have listened to my gut and not trusted her.

CHAPTER 14

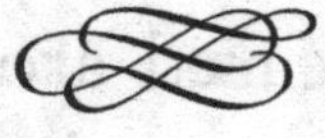

As I approached Sage Advice, I noticed a tall, lanky man walking around the building. I couldn't make out his features since the sun had already set.

Instead of confronting him, I stilled and watched him for a bit, wondering who the heck it could be.

He paced the front of the building, then held up his phone. I squinted, attempting to see the screen, but it was futile.

When I'd played Cassie, I'd blown up a rapist's home by placing explosives along the foundation, then hitting the detonator as I walked away. It had been an epic explosion on the green screen and one of the most watched episodes. Social media had gone wild with women thanking the network for finally giving the villain what he deserved. This guy reminded me of when I set the explosives as he bent over and began tapping the foundation.

When he disappeared around the side of the building, I hurried over and waited for him at the front door. A few moments later, he startled as he rounded the other corner.

"You scared me!" he exclaimed, his phone lighting up his face. Probably in his thirties, he wore a thick black beard and glasses. Tattoos peeked out from under the collar of his shirt and jacket. "What can I do for you?"

"I was wondering what I can do for you before I call the police," I replied, crossing my arms over my chest. "I live here."

His eyes widened but he quickly rearranged his features and plastered on a friendly smile. "I'm with Chester Development Corporation." He stuck out his hand. "My name's Aiden. We weren't aware anyone lived in the property since the owner died."

I ignored his attempted handshake. Rude, yes, but I was at my wits' end for the day. "What do you want?"

"Well, it's our understanding the will is to be

read next week, and we've assumed the building is going to the next of kin. We're going to place an offer. I wanted to check the measurements so we know what we're buying."

How presumptuous. "Oh, really. What makes you think the new owner will want to sell?"

He smiled. "Money is a great motivator."

I didn't bother to tell him I was the new owner, and I wouldn't sell, no matter how much money he offered me. I'd been wealthy before and it had brought me misery. By keeping Sage Advice, I had a stable future and something meaningful not only to me, but to many in Heywood and the surrounding area. Besides, I'd made a promise to Bonnie by accepting her offer, and I never went back on a promise.

"Why do you want the building?"

"We've been looking for another location for a resort. My company specializes in bringing new industry to underdeveloped towns. Heywood seems like the perfect place." He stretched his hands out to each side. "If we can buy this building and the two on each side, it would be an amazing location for a hotel, especially with the views."

I snorted and shook my head. "I don't think anyone in town wants your resort." I certainly didn't. "Sometimes, things are best left the way they are."

He furrowed his brow in confusion. "Why wouldn't the people appreciate the hotel? It would be a big boon for the economy."

I hadn't been in Heywood long, but I definitely got the vibe that the citizens of this idyllic little town were perfectly happy being stuck in time. Heck, take Annabelle for example. She was reliving the 80s everyday! "A lot of people think the economy is fine just the way it is."

"Well, we'll see about that. Money talks. My guess is that we'll own this building by the end of the month at the latest."

Over my dead body. "For tonight, I live here, so I would appreciate you leaving the premises," I said, suddenly dead tired. Catnip and a glass of Chardonnay waited for me upstairs.

"I just wanted to grab a few more measurements if you don't mind. Unfortunately, I would suggest that you start looking for a new place to live."

Unable to believe the audacity of the man, I simply stared at him as my anger boiled to the surface. "I suggest you get off the property," I hissed. "And I can promise you, you'll never own this building if I have anything to say about it.

Now go before I have you arrested for trespassing."

He opened his mouth to argue, but instead, he turned on his heel, slid into his Tesla parked on the street, and drove away.

With a long sigh, I opened the door, then locked it behind me once I was inside. I didn't bother with the lights as I made my way past the display tables, through the back room, and up the stairs. Catnip greeted me at my apartment door, meowing loudly and weaving between my legs once again as I walked to the kitchen. Was he trying to trip me up?

Finally settled against the couch cushions with my Chardonnay, I felt the world closing in on me. I both relished the reading of the will next week and hoped it never came. It would bring me a tidal wave of drama and I wasn't quite ready for it, but I doubted I'd ever be prepared to face Catherine's wrath.

When my phone rang, I grabbed it off the coffee table and answered.

"Ms. Jones, this is Colin Breckshire, III. I hope it's not too late to call."

"Not at all," I replied, sitting up. "What can I do for you?"

"I was wondering if you'll be attending the reading of the will next week?"

I'd rather shave my eyebrows, but if need be, I'd attend. "Do I *have* to be there?"

"Of course not. And, I was going to suggest that it may be best if you didn't."

"Why is that?"

"Well, I'm under the impression that things will get quite contentious with Bonnie's daughter. Let's just say Bonnie has told me stories. I think it would be best if she didn't have a direct target to lash out at."

"That target being me."

"Yes, especially since you've agreed to Bonnie's terms and are willing to keep the store."

"I'd be happy to skip it." The last thing I needed was a psychopath screaming at me in a lawyer's office. "I didn't think people actually held a reading of a will any longer."

"It's an antiquated practice, but Bonnie requested it."

"She did? When she knew Catherine would be so upset?"

"Oh, yes," Breckshire said, chuckling. "There was no love lost between Bonnie and Catherine. It'll be quite the scene as Bonnie has a few surprises lined up for those in attendance."

Another peek into Bonnie's mean side. Personally, I thought her plan bordered on cruel, but I'd never had children, let alone one I didn't like and who stole from me.

Breckshire sounded as if he was looking forward to the melee, but I didn't question him. Some people thrived on drama, others didn't. Personally, I'd had enough both onscreen and off to last me a lifetime.

"Well, thank you," I said. "I appreciate the call."

"Ms. Jones, if you don't mind me asking, who will be handling the transfer of the business into your name?"

I'd given it a bit of thought, and it seemed using someone familiar with the affairs would be my best option. "Well, I was hoping you would, but I wasn't sure if that would be a conflict of interest."

"Not at all. It would be smart of you since I'm well-versed in all of Bonnie's business dealings."

"Then yes, let's do that."

"Perfect. I'll call you next week after I've drawn up all the paperwork. Have a wonderful night, Ms. Jones."

"You, too."

I set my phone onto the cushion next to me. At least, I now had a lawyer.

With a laugh, I stood and poured myself some more wine. Next week would be terrible—no doubt about it. Catherine would discover she's no longer going to get her yoga studio and become unhinged. That seemed to be her style. Annabelle would most likely be quite surprised I was the heir, especially if she was somehow working with Catherine. I'd have to deal with Aiden again as he tried to sweettalk me into selling. Doctor Butte would be furious when he found out I had no plans to change anything about Sage Advice. In fact, I had some ideas about expansion.

The business was now my baby, and no one would take it away from me.

I turned on reruns of *Friends* and thought about all the people who were about to have their world turned upside down. Bonnie had really left a mess in her wake. The wake. That's right. I was supposed to find out if there was a funeral.

After picking up the phone, I called Breckshire back.

"What can I do for you, Ms. Jones?"

"Is there anything in the will about a funeral?" I asked. "When it is... where it is? Any details about what Bonnie wanted?"

"Yes. There's very detailed information. A private family service will be held tomorrow. There won't be a public service."

"Where's the family service being held?"

"At the church. Eleven in the morning."

"Did Bonnie have siblings?" I tried to think of exactly who would be considered family, and the only one I could think of was Catherine.

"Yes. Two sisters, both deceased. Tomorrow, the Tuppers will be there, as will Catherine and one of Bonnie's cousins."

I'd almost forgotten that Charlie and Bonnie were Catherine's parents. "How do you know they'll all be there?"

"Because Bonnie specified in her will that if they didn't attend the service, they wouldn't be eligible for any inheritance."

Wow. That seemed a bit much. "Okay, thanks."

"We'll speak soon, Ms. Jones."

I set down my phone again and stared at the television, not really hearing what was being said, but I knew Ross and Rachel were on a break. Instead, my mind churned. When I'd gone to the Tuppers' farm, Charlie had mentioned how expensive it was to run the place. *It's been in my family for a few generations. Costs a pretty penny to run it, though.*

Had Bonnie left him anything?

I phoned Breckshire again. "I'm sorry to bother you," I said without preamble. "Just out of curiosity, did Bonnie leave Charlie Tupper anything in her will?"

"I'm afraid I can't disclose that."

Closing my eyes, I pushed my glasses up my nose. "Mr. Breckshire, I already know Catherine is going to be quite upset by Bonnie leaving me the store. There will be words between us. I'm just wondering if I need to expect Charlie to turn on me as well."

A long stretch of silence ensued, then he said, "I don't think so, Ms. Jones. Bonnie left Charlie Tupper thirty thousand dollars. He should be quite satisfied with that."

"Did he know she was going to do that?"

"She mentioned that she was going to tell him, but I'm not sure if she ever did."

I sat back against the cushions and nodded. "Thanks so much."

After hanging up, I stared at the floor and absently ran my hand over Catnip's back. Would thirty thousand dollars go a long way on a farm? I had to assume that if it didn't, it would most certainly help.

Costs a pretty penny to run it, though.

What if Bonnie had mentioned her intentions to Charlie, and he'd killed her?

I groaned and laid my head back, staring at the ceiling. My ruminations weren't getting me any closer to finding the killer. They only added more suspects to my list.

CHAPTER 15

THE NEXT MORNING, I went for a run on the Riverwalk, hoping to catch Doug coherent and sober.

I found him sitting in the sun next to his bridge, reading.

"Doug!" I called as I approached.

"Sam! Great to see you!" He stood and wiped his hands on his trousers, then set his book down on the pathway next to his foot. I read the title as I attempted to catch my breath. Your Mind on Plants by Michael Pollan. "How is it?" I asked, pointing at the tome.

"Very interesting. I think you'll want to read this one since you work with herbs and such."

I nodded, mentally adding the book to my

long reading list. Bonnie had left me dozens to help me in my herbalist journey. "I'm glad you're okay. You were certainly out of it last time I saw you."

"That was you?"

Placing my hands on my hips, I took a deep breath. "What do you mean?"

"You're the one who put a blanket over me and turned me to my side."

"Yes. That was indeed me." And I'd thought he'd been completely unconscious, but I'd been wrong.

"Thank you," he said. "You're very kind. I've been meaning to come see you."

"What for?" I hoped it was to ask for help in getting off the drugs, but sharing with me that he recalled seeing the murderer would be even better.

"I remember someone on the path the day Bonnie died."

Just as I succeeded in bringing my heartrate down, it amped back up again. "Who? Are you sure?"

"Pretty sure," he said hesitantly while he ran his hand over his beard.

"Who?"

"The girl who works with you. The one responsible for the hole in the ozone layer with all the hairspray she uses."

"Annabelle?"

"Yes."

"You saw Annabelle that morning?"

He nodded. "I remembered her and Bonnie walking together. Bonnie had on a pink hat and I thought she looked awfully spring-ish for it being fall."

I longed to question Doug about his thought processes but refrained. There was no way for me to understand his mind. "Are you absolutely certain you saw Annabelle with Bonnie that morning?"

"Not a hundred percent, but I'm fairly confident."

"So it could've been another day?"

"Maybe... but I think it was that day."

"Were they arguing?"

"I don't know," he replied, shrugging. "I didn't pay close attention to them."

Something was off. He recalled Bonnie's hat and equated it to spring, but he couldn't recall if they were arguing? If they had been and the conversation had been heated enough for Annabelle to kill Bonnie, it would've been memorable.

At least to someone who wasn't on drugs.

"Do you remember anything else?" I asked.

He shook his head. "No. Just I noticed Annabelle and Bonnie that morning strolling along the Riverwalk."

"Okay, thanks," I muttered. "Have a good day, Doug."

As I continued my jog, I wondered why Annabelle hadn't told me she'd seen Bonnie that morning. Either Doug had been mistaken on the date, or Annabelle had killed her and was trying to cover it up.

At the end of the Riverwalk, the geese eyed me while I climbed the path leading to the street. Then, an idea hit me on my way back to Sage Advice.

It wasn't a smart one, but it may shed some light on who had killed Bonnie. I picked up my pace and arrived at the store before Annabelle. After a quick shower, I texted her.

Funeral for Bonnie is today, but we aren't invited. Family only. And I was going to be there, so I needed to lie to Annabelle on my whereabouts. *Have a couple of errands to run. You okay by yourself for a few hours?*

I waited for her to answer, although she'd have to be fine on her own whether she liked it or not.

Yes.

Okay. With the store covered, I could put my plan into action.

As I was about to leave, my phone rang. Tinkering on Trucks. Finally, news on my car.

"Hey, Harry," I said. "What's going on?"

"First, I wanted to apologize for the delay in getting back to you. My daughter and wife both have had the flu this week, and I haven't been at the shop as much as I usually am. I'm a bit behind on things."

"Your family should come first," I replied. "I hope they're feeling better."

"Thanks. About your car…"

Please be totaled. Please be totaled. "What is it?"

"Well, the thing is wrecked and should be scrapped," he said. "I'm going to let the insurance company know. But Sam… the cops were here yesterday looking at it."

My blood ran cold while the room suddenly became claustrophobic. I took a deep breath and tried to calm my thundering heart. "Did they say why?"

"No. They were tight-lipped. Just went through the car, then left."

"Did you happen to get the name of the person who was there?"

"Yeah, it was the sheriff. Mallory's her name."

I shut my eyes for a brief moment. Her actions made no sense. Bonnie had been killed the day after my accident. Why was Mallory looking at my car? How could she think it had something to do with Bonnie's death?

"Thanks, Harry," I muttered. "I guess the next step is the insurance company will call me?"

"Right. Is everything okay? Why were the police here?"

I contemplated what to say, then shook my head. "I have no idea. That's my answer to both questions."

After hanging up, I made myself a green smoothie. Mallory would have to know Harry would call me and tell me she'd been there. Was she really searching the car because she thought it was somehow involved in the murder, which would show an epic level of incompetence, or was she trying to scare me? Make me aware she was sniffing around in every aspect of my life, whether it had anything to do with the murder or not?

Instead of trying to sort her intentions, I focused on the task in front of me. The funeral would be starting soon, and I needed to get into place.

"Be a good boy, Catnip," I said, closing the door and dashing down the stairs.

After locking up the building, I hurried up to the church. I hadn't been in one in decades, and I momentarily worried I'd be struck down upon entering.

The stone structure, according to the plaque outside, had been built for use as a Catholic church hundreds of years ago when Heywood had been discovered, but was now non-denominational and all were welcome. I opened the thick, wooden door to find two rows of wooden pews, large stained-glass windows, and past the altar area, ceiling-to-floor windows offering a magnificent view of the river and beyond.

"Oh, wow," I whispered, wishing I had time to enjoy it. Instead, I glanced around and wondered what side I should choose. Instinctively, I would sit on the right, so I hurried over to the second pew from the back on the left, sank to my knees, and shimmied under the seat. Closing my eyes, I sent up a little prayer I wouldn't be found, because I had no idea how to explain myself.

The service was supposed to start at eleven. At quarter till, no one had come into the church, but I had heard people moving about up front, which I had to assume was church staff getting everything ready. What if no one showed to celebrate Bonnie's life?

But a few minutes before eleven, the doors opened and, from my vantage point, I spotted a pair of black high heels. The way she marched down the aisle led me to believe it was Catherine. A few moments later, the door swung open again and I noted cowboy boots and sensible flats. Most likely the Tuppers. Trailing behind them, more practical shoes and a walker. Bonnie's cousin, I assumed. Then a set of dark, men's loafers walked by. I had no idea who their owner may be.

"Welcome, everyone," a deep voice said. Minister Paul, I presumed. In his twenties and more handsome than the day is long, he reminded me of a young Paul Rudd, who I'd met once and found just as charming as he appeared in interviews. "We're here to celebrate Bonnie's life."

As he spoke, I couldn't help but think it had been prepared remarks, already handed to him. They flowed too well, having too much detail for a minister to pull together. Had Bonnie written her own memorial as well?

"One of Bonnie's greatest achievements was to remain friends with her former lover, Charlie Tupper, and she felt so blessed Doreen Tupper also accepted their relationship and their daughter, Catherine. Bonnie appreciated the parental team the three of you made."

Someone snorted and whispered something under their breath. I imagined it to be Catherine.

Minister Paul continued, saying that some of Bonnie's joys in life included helping people and giving to animal shelters. "As a big believer in second chances and starting over, Bonnie took many under her wing looking to embark on a different path from what they'd previously traveled. This was her passion. Recognizing the good in everyone, and helping those in need."

Tears welled in my eyes as I lay under the dusty pew. Bonnie had been so kind to me the day I'd walked into Sage Advice, desperate and in need of a new start—and she'd given it to me. What had she seen in me that day? What had prompted her to hire someone who was only a hobby herbalist, when the job had required so much more?

"Does anyone have anything they'd like to say?" Minister Paul asked.

"Bonnie was a wonderful woman. One I'll miss," a soft voice said which I didn't recognize. "She always came to stay with me in Florida for two weeks during the winter. We had a wonderful time together." *Must be the cousin.*

Charlie cleared his throat. "Bonnie and I had our ups and downs, but we remained dedicated to raising Catherine. And we agreed to do it without all the fighting and bickering you sometimes find with parents who aren't together. Through it all we remained good friends. I loved her in my own way and respected her greatly. I'll miss her."

"Oh, for the love of God... can we just all stop the lies?" Catherine said. "My mother was a horrible woman and I'm glad she's dead!"

Silence fell over the church for a long moment, then Doreen spoke. "Catherine, she wasn't horrible. *You're* the problem in every relationship you have. You've stolen from not only your father, but from Bonnie as well. Did you think for a moment we'd like to retire, and you taking your father's money would prevent that from happening? Did you think Bonnie would have liked to spend her last years slaving away in the store? Bonnie wasn't the issue, Catherine. Take a look in the mirror."

Catherine let out a string of words that shouldn't be spoken in any church, regardless of denomination. "Shut up, Doreen. You're no better than Bonnie, so save your self-righteous indignation for someone who gives two nickels."

"How dare you!" Doreen yelled.

"I know you and Charlie killed her. The farm's going under!" Catherine screamed. "Everyone knows! You're hoping to get your grubby hands on some of her money, but it's not going to happen. She told me she's left me everything. Did you hear me? *Everything*! And I plan to keep every cent and watch you two become homeless! Maybe that creep under the bridge will take you in!"

"I doubt she left you two pennies to rub together," Doreen muttered.

"We'll see," Catherine hissed. "I've fulfilled Bonnie's request to attend this sham of a memorial, and now, I'm leaving." She stormed out of the church.

I let out a breath that I hadn't realized I'd been holding. In my mind, Catherine's behavior only solidified she must have killed her mother. I felt like I needed a shower, and it wasn't from the dust under the pew. Catherine's vitriol settled on my skin like oil.

"I'm sorry, Minister," Charlie said. "I apologize for her outburst."

"If I may, Mr. Tupper... your daughter is a full-grown woman. Her actions are her own. If anyone should apologize for her behavior, it's her, not you."

"Thank you, sir," Charlie replied. "Just not sure how she turned out the way she did."

As they spoke for a few more minutes, I hoped they'd wrap it up soon. Not only was I having a hot flash, but I also had to use the restroom. Menopause was awesome and seemed to strike at the least opportune times.

Thankfully, the service ended moments later and everyone cleared out of the church. Who in the world did those loafers belong to? Obviously, no one involved in the family drama, because they'd remained quiet throughout the shouting. I waited until the silence became deafening, then slid out from under the pew and peeked around the corner to make sure I was alone.

I stood and hurried outside, glad I'd taken the risk of sneaking into the church. According to Catherine, the farm was going under. Sounded like the perfect motive for murder.

Charlie and Bonnie had remained close for decades. Perhaps at one time they'd had a conversation about wills and leaving money. Had Charlie helped Bonnie's demise along out of desperation over losing the farm?

But then, Catherine also believed she had a large stake in Bonnie's estate.

Money.

It had ruined my life and now it appeared Bonnie's had ended because of it.

Maybe it was the root of all evil.

CHAPTER 16

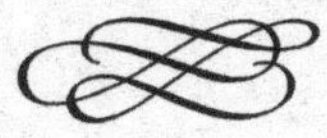

OVER THE NEXT FEW DAYS, I longed to speak to Catherine face to face, but I was unsure what to say to her. *Did you kill your mother? Did you hire someone to do it? Are you really that coldblooded?*

But I didn't think those questions would go over well. I'd most likely end up with a fist in my face. Even so, I searched her out, but I could never find her. I even checked the motel and bed and breakfast and came up with zilch. Unless the owners were lying, Catherine wasn't staying in town. After debating whether she'd be shacking up at Charlie's place, I firmly decided that after what I'd witnessed in the church, neither would want anything to do with the other.

While out the day before the reading of the will,

I noted File It Away had their open sign showing, so I popped in to see Gina and ask after the puppies.

"Hey, you!" she said from behind the glass counter, shoving a grape in her mouth. "Come in. Are you here for your nails?"

I shook my head.

"Well, you should be, but I've got a client in ten minutes and don't have time for you right now. So, what's up?"

I snickered, appreciating her honesty. "I've been thinking about the puppies and wondering how they were doing."

"They're cuter than you can imagine," she said, tucking a lock of blonde hair behind her ear. "The birth took forever, but it went well, and everyone is healthy."

"That's great. I'm so happy to hear it." And I was. I'd been consumed with worry about being arrested for Bonnie's murder and trying to figure out who'd really killed her. Hearing about innocent puppies soothed me.

"You sure you don't want one?"

"No, thanks. I can barely take care of myself and Bonnie's cat. A puppy would send me over the edge."

"Do you want to see some pictures?" she

asked, pulling out her phone, not bothering to wait for an answer. Who didn't want to ooh and aww over puppy photos? "They're the cutest things ever." She turned the screen toward me. "Like I told you, Mama's a lab. Not sure what Dad was, but they made beautiful babies."

Little brown and white balls of fluff curled up against the mom as she stared into the camera with her tongue hanging out, almost as if she was thrilled with her creations. "They're darlings," I said. Honestly, I wasn't sure which won the cuteness award: the puppies or the dwarf cows at the Tupper farm.

"See? You need one," Gina teased.

"I really don't. But thank you."

"Do you have kids?" she asked, tucking away her phone into her back pocket. "A husband? If so, you definitely need a dog."

I shook my head and almost mentioned that I'd been too focused on my previous career to raise a family, but quickly caught myself. "I don't have a nurturing bone in my body. I wouldn't make a good mother." It was partially true, at least when I was of childbearing age. Now, with menopause setting in, I probably didn't have the patience, either. "My husband died." But not before he ruined my life. Hello, bitterness, my old friend.

"My ex-husband is the worst man in the world and if he died tomorrow, I wouldn't shed a tear," she said, picking another grape out of her bowl. "We had one kid, my son. Thankfully, he's nothing like his father and a nice guy. I'll take full credit for his demeanor because his father's a scumbag. My boy graduates next year and I'm not sure what I'm going to do with myself. Probably get another dog. They're loyal, they don't talk back, and they actually listen every now and then, unlike husbands and kids."

"Is your son going to college?" I asked, snickering at her dig on husbands. We'd both chosen badly.

"He doesn't know yet. Says he wants to be an actor, but I'm hoping he doesn't choose the route. From what I've read, it's nothing but heartache, rejection, and poverty for ninety-nine percent of them. We'll get it figured out."

How right she was. The more time I spent with Gina, the more I liked her. Smart, brutally honest, and down-to-earth. "Listen, I was wondering if you've seen Catherine around lately? The one with the broken nail I asked you about?"

She shook her head. "Nope. But I haven't been open much because of the puppies."

I sighed and glanced around the store, not sure what to do next. Perhaps have that conversation with Annabelle I'd been putting off?

"When are you going to let me get my hands on your nails?" Gina asked.

I glanced down at my fingertips. They didn't look *that* bad. Besides, I'd made a promise to myself to leave all the fluff behind and live authentically. "How about I take you for a coffee instead?" The words left my mouth before I could process them. What the heck was wrong with me? Was I subconsciously attempting to develop a relationship?

"That would be great!" Gina said, glancing over my shoulder to the door. "Let me know when." She reached to the shelf behind her and grabbed a business card, then plunked it down on the counter between us. "Call me."

After picking it up, I nodded and pivoted to leave the store, almost crashing into the woman entering.

We exchanged pleasantries, and I returned to Sage Advice to find Annabelle hunched over a worktable in back, adding alcohol to some herbs to make a tincture.

"Hi," she said, not looking up from her work. "I had another idea for the store."

And once again, she brought up future plans for Sage Advice, which really bothered me since she didn't know who the new owner would be. Yes, she mentioned that she was manifesting what she wanted. But her actions all seemed a little suspect to me, especially when Doug had mentioned he thought he'd seen her with Bonnie the morning she'd been killed.

"What's that?" I asked, pulling out the inventory clipboard. Today, Annabelle wore a neon green and pink tracksuit with pink tennis shoes, her hair in its usual ten-inch salute.

"An online store," she said, meeting my gaze, her eyes shining with excitement. "We could ship almost all of our inventory and become an international company, not just a local one."

I smiled, appreciating her thought process. "Great minds think alike," I said. "I had the same idea." And, I'd looked into online merchants and made a note to mention it to Breckshire to explore what was involved in the legal and tax realms.

Annabelle squealed with happiness, shaking her fist. "Oh, my gosh. It's kismet. We're going to be able to continue to work at the store. I can feel it my bones, Sam! Heck, maybe one of us will even inherit it!"

What an interesting thing to say. Her excitement radiated off her, and I wanted to soak it all in, to allow it to wash over me and infect me as it had her. But no. I still didn't trust her, and I wasn't sure how to bypass that without knowing who killed Bonnie. "You think so?"

"I'm praying for it," she replied as she went back to her tincture.

I glanced over her shoulder at the mason jar. "What are you making?"

"An anxiety tincture," she murmured. "It'll be ready in about six weeks." After twisting on the lid, she wrote *Anxiety* on a label, listed the contents and the date, then set the glass container up on the shelf.

I hurried into the front room and did a quick count of our dry herbs and soap baskets. Everyone seemed to love the lavender basket consisting of soap, body lotion, and hair oil. We'd run out once again. "Annabelle?" I called.

She stuck her head around the corner. "Yes?"

"We need more lavender soap baskets. When do you think is the best time for us to make those?" Creating soap was somewhat time consuming and shouldn't be interrupted, so we had to do it when the store was closed.

"How about tomorrow morning before we open? I can come in a little early."

"Perfect. Between the two of us, I think we should be able to more than double our production."

"Sounds good." She disappeared into the back room again and I finished up the inventory.

We made an excellent team, and it would be even better if I could get past my distrust. Deciding to tackle the problem directly, I went into the back room, returned the clipboard to its hook on the wall, and pulled up a stool next to her. She stared at me expectantly.

"Who do you think killed Bonnie?" I asked.

Glancing around the workroom, she shrugged and shook her head. "I have no idea. If I had to guess, it would be Catherine. Or even Doctor Butte. He'd been fighting with Bonnie for years. Maybe he finally had enough of her besting him."

Fair enough. I'd had the same thoughts many times.

"Who do you think did it?" she asked.

"I have no idea." Well, I did have a couple of thoughts on the matter, but I wouldn't share them with her quite yet. Not until I could trust her.

The arrows still flashed in Annabelle's direction, and I had to clear the air for my own sanity. Did I expect a confession? No. But maybe she'd say something to put my mind at ease.

I took a deep breath, then blurted, "Someone told me they saw you walking with Bonnie the morning she was killed."

I studied her response. Her eyes widened and she quickly looked away.

"Is it true?" I asked, assuming by her reaction that it was.

"Who told you that?"

"It doesn't matter." I wouldn't throw Doug under the bus. "Is it true, Annabelle?"

She swallowed as tears tracked down her cheeks. "Yes," she whispered.

Finally, a little more progress in finding Bonnie's killer. "Can you tell me what happened?"

"We got an early morning coffee, talked about the store a bit, then went for a walk along the river."

"What happened between you two, Annabelle?"

"Nothing!" she said, throwing her hands up. "We were walking along and I thought I may have left my curling iron on. I left her to go home and check and told her I'd see her at the store."

I recalled that morning and her story didn't add up. "Annabelle, that day when we were looking for her, you never mentioned any of this."

"It didn't seem important that I'd been with her before she died."

"You went upstairs and looked in her apartment," I continued. "Like you had no idea where she could've been."

"I thought maybe she'd beaten me back to the shop. Or, she'd come home and left again for some appointment she didn't tell me about."

With a sigh, I pushed my glasses up my nose as a headache began to form behind my eyes. "Why didn't you tell any of this to the police?"

She remained silent for a long moment, not meeting my gaze. "Because I was afraid."

"Of what?"

"That they'd think I did it. I was one of the last people to see her alive."

And there it was. Annabelle held back important information from the cops because of her fears that she'd be a suspect. Which was exactly what I should have done, come to think of it. If I hadn't shared my letter with Jordan, I wouldn't be on Mallory's radar and I'd only be worrying about my past being revealed instead of going to prison for a crime I didn't commit.

"Did you see anyone on the path after you left?" I asked.

"Loads of people," she said. "There was a walking tour going on."

I recalled seeing one as well. "Anyone who would want to hurt Bonnie?"

She shook her head. "I really wasn't paying attention."

We sat in silence for a long while, the unasked question hanging between us.

I took a deep breath. "Annabelle, did you kill Bonnie?"

"No," she whispered. "I swear to you, I didn't."

I wanted to believe her, but I also had wanted to believe my husband wasn't capable of defrauding my friends and colleagues out of millions and millions of dollars. That confidence in him had been misplaced, and I feared the same with Annabelle.

"I'll swear on any Bible you want," she said, raising her left hand. I didn't bother to correct her that she should be lifting her right.

My experience of playing the devilish Cassie rose to the surface once again. I could go to the police with this new information and take the investigational spotlight off of me, or at least have Annabelle join me in it. One of us was inheriting the store. The other was the last to see her alive and wanted the store so badly, she was making future plans.

But then again, if Annabelle had killed her, why would she admit to being with her that morning? Doug could've very well had the wrong day and she could've denied it—her word against a drug addict's. There wouldn't even be a question as to who the police would believe.

"Are you going to tell the cops?" she asked.

I hadn't made up my mind, so I simply shrugged.

"Please, Sam. Don't. I'm begging you."

"What about Catherine?" I asked. "Someone also saw you talking to her outside the nail salon. Why?"

She smiled innocently. "I told her to stay away from the store because she had horrible juju."

Was it that simple? Had she warned off Catherine, or had they been working together on Bonnie's murder?

All the evidence pointed to it. First, Annabelle was one of the last people to see Bonnie alive, and she'd hidden that piece of knowledge from the police. Second, she'd spoken to Catherine, and

Gina had said it wasn't a heated conversation. A collusion of some sort?

I needed to protect myself, not just from the investigation, but from Annabelle herself, and I wasn't quite sure how to do that. Should I turn her in to the police? Tell them everything I knew? Or lay low a little while longer and see how everything played out?

If she was the murderer, or she and Catherine were in on it together, and thought I could bring her down, I'd have to watch my back closer than ever.

CHAPTER 17

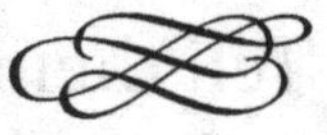

THE BIG DAY HAD ARRIVED: the reading of the will. The day everyone would know that I now owned the store, and I expected to hear from almost every single person who had been invited to the event.

"It's going to be an ugly day, Catnip," I said as I tried to run a comb through my curls. "People are going to be upset, which I fully understand, but I hope they don't take it out on me."

The feline eyed me from the doorway of the bathroom, his tail swishing back and forth as I fought my hair. My grays seemed more pronounced in the natural light filtering through the small window above the shower. I'd heard them once referred to as wisdom highlights, so I planned to stick with that description.

"I can only hope everything will settle down after this," I said, giving up on one tangle and throwing the comb into the basket. Not only did my nails require some care, but I also apparently needed a haircut. "Then I can get back to my quiet, unassuming life. Doesn't that sound good, Catnip?"

He meowed and stalked from the room. After brushing my teeth, I found him nestled among the pillows of my unmade bed.

"I'll be up to check on you later. Don't get in trouble, okay?"

Yesterday, I'd come home to find the roll of bagels I'd left out on the counter ripped open and he'd taken a bite off each one. Why not just eat a full one? Why be a passive-aggressive jerk and ruin them all? I'd threatened to kick him out, but he only stared at me from under hooded lids, ready to call my bluff. Having him around had grown on me and he knew as well as I did it was an empty warning.

I headed downstairs and began my day. A little dusting. Checking the dates on the tinctures and dividing the ready ones into smaller dropper bottles. Printing labels and fixing them to the proper product. All the while, I hummed softly and wondered if Catnip would behave himself if I allowed him to free-roam the store. It had to get pretty boring sitting upstairs all day, even for a cat who seemed perfectly happy to perch on the back of the couch and stare out the window for most of the daylight hours.

When Annabelle came in, she smiled and waved as if our conversation the previous afternoon had never occurred. As if I'd never asked if she'd committed murder. I found her cheerful demeanor a bit unnerving, and I hoped she didn't have any plans to stick a knife in my back.

"Ready to make some soap?" she asked as she pulled an apron off the hook on the wall. Today, her clothing resembled something out of Madonna's early closet, including loads of bracelets, a bandana around her crimped hair, and bright red lipstick. "We've got plenty of lavender essential oil, so we can make as many as you think we need."

I wasn't sure what that amount was, and I voiced my ignorance. One thing Bonnie had always stressed was to have fresh inventory. It didn't matter what the product—soap, tinctures, or capsules—they should always be fresh.

"I don't think we should have a bunch of it sitting around," Annabelle said. "But let's stick to our original plan and double what we made last time and see how long it lasts."

"Sounds good."

"Would you mind if we listened to a little Duran Duran? Their album, *Rio*, always puts me in a good mood."

"Have at it," I said, tempted to tell her about when I met Simon Le Bon at a party and the shenanigans that ensued, but I decided against it. Maybe some other time when I was convinced she wasn't Bonnie's killer.

After she pulled an old boom box from a lower cupboard, she scoured her purse, eventually extracting a cassette. She snapped it into the tape player and hit rewind.

"That's… that's really old school, Annabelle." When was the last time I'd seen a working boom box? I couldn't recall.

"There's no better way to be," she replied, giggling.

An hour later, we sang and danced along to "Hungry Like the Wolf" and the soap was setting in the molds. Forgetting about the murder even for a short period of time did wonders for my mood until someone knocked on the front door just as my phone rang.

"I'll get the door, you answer your phone," Annabelle said, turning off the boom box. "And thanks for agreeing to the music. Bonnie always hated it, but it really makes me happy. Brings back the youth I loved so much."

"Of course," I called out as she hurried into the front room, making a mental note to add more music to our days in the future, if Annabelle wasn't rotting in prison for killing Bonnie. I really hoped she was innocent because I had no idea how to find a qualified herbalist to help me with the store. Glancing at my screen, I recognized Breckshire's number. "Hello?"

"Hello, Ms. Jones. I'm sorry to bother you, but I wanted to let you know that the reading of Bonnie's will has been completed. As expected, not everyone was pleased. I heard your name mentioned a few times and I wanted to give you fair warning that you may have some visitors."

"Where is she?!"

I glanced at the doorway to the front room, recognizing Catherine's booming voice.

"Thanks for the heads up," I replied. "They've arrived."

"If I may, who's there?"

Peeking around the corner, I said, "Catherine,

Charlie and Doreen, and Doctor Butte. Was he at the reading?"

"Yes, he was. She wanted him to hear from her firsthand that Sage Advice would continue to operate."

I recalled the loafers at Bonnie's memorial and now realized they must have belonged to Butte. Bonnie had insisted anyone who was listed in the reading of the will had to attend her memorial or they'd be cut out of any inheritance. Dang, Bonnie did have a mean streak.

"Get her out here now!" Catherine yelled.

"Calm down!" Charlie replied. "Stop acting like a crazy banshee on drugs!"

"I better go," I said. "They're fighting, and I'm afraid Catherine's going to tear the store apart."

"For your safety and the sake of Sage Advice, I'm calling the police," Breckshire announced. I didn't argue. "I'll be in touch soon, Ms. Jones."

As I shoved my phone into my back pocket, I took a deep breath. I couldn't lose my temper, but I wouldn't be pushed around, either. Rounding the corner, I set my shoulders back and narrowed my gaze. When I exchanged glances with Annabelle, she smirked, muttering, "Oh, no. Cassie's in the house. This is about to get interesting."

"What can I do for you, Catherine," I asked, eyeing the woman while crossing my arms over my chest. I realized that all the suspects were gathered in the store, except for Doug. Maybe the murder could be solved in a matter of moments if I could get someone to confess. It was time to bait them… to make them angry enough so they'd reveal their secrets.

"You can get out of my store!" she shrieked. "This is supposed to be mine!"

"Apparently, your mother didn't see it that way. But since you obviously thought you'd benefit from her death, I have to ask… Did you kill your own mother, Catherine? Are you that callous and greedy?"

She stared at me a long moment, her eyes wide with fury and surprise. "Of course not! What a horrible thing to say!"

"From what I've heard, you're more than capable."

Silence fell over the room as she stared at me. I'd hit a nerve.

"You're an ugly human," she whispered. "I may not have liked my mother—I actually hated her—but I'd never kill her."

Fair enough. "But you would sneak around in her apartment at night, right? And maybe push someone down who was only trying to take care of the cat?"

Her gaze flickered for a brief second, and I had my answer.

"That's what I thought."

"I was looking for the will!" Catherine wailed.

"Of course, you were. Forget mourning your mother or taking care of her belongings. *You*, Catherine, are the ugly human being." We stared at each other a long moment. "Now, unless you'd like to purchase something, please leave *my* store."

Annabelle gasped. Glancing over at her, I found her staring at me wide-eyed with her hand over her mouth, not even trying to hide her shock. She hadn't missed my announcement that I was now the owner.

I turned to Butte. "And what can I do for you?"

"Bonnie requested I be at the reading of her will. I was told she was leaving me something and in order to receive it, I had to be there. Come to find out, she wanted me to know the store wasn't going anywhere. I came here to tell you that neither am I. I'll fight to have you closed down until the day I die. Your plants put people's lives in danger."

"If you stopped writing prescriptions for a few

hours and actually read up on how herbs heal, you may be surprised," I shot back. "And just out of curiosity, did she leave you anything?"

His face reddened as his hands fisted at his sides. "Yes. She left me exactly six dollars and sixty-six cents."

Annabelle gasped again while Catherine snorted, then said, "The symbol of Satan himself. She wasn't too far off on that."

With a sigh, I rolled my eyes and ignored Catherine, although I fully agreed with her. I was also secretly impressed with Bonnie's last dig at Butte. "We should be working as one, Doctor. Traditional and herbal medicines can function together to bring wonderful results."

"Never," he hissed, pointing at me. "You and I aren't done."

"Is that a threat?" I asked. "Were you so scared of Bonnie and the relief her plants gave people that you had to kill her?"

He arched an eyebrow and gritted his teeth. "I've already told you. I'm a doctor. I live by the rule of 'do no harm.'"

"And I think you're a snake in the grass drug peddler," I said. "You can attempt to intimidate me all you want, Butte, but you'll be sorry in the end."

"Are *you* threatening *me*?"

I smiled and shook my head. "You can take it any way you'd like. I prefer to think of it as more of a promise, though."

Glancing over at Charlie and Doreen, he stared at me as if I'd grown another head, while she cried silent tears.

"Can we please stop this bickering?" she sniffled. "Bonnie's dead. Her legacy has been set in stone. Some aren't happy, but there's no use in arguing about it. There's nothing further to do."

Charlie took her into an embrace and she cried against his chest, while little whimpers emanated from her.

"Are you all done?" I asked. "Doreen's right. You're all angry that you didn't get what you wanted. It happens to people every single day. Get over yourselves and move on with your lives."

A police cruiser pulled up front and Jordan exited the vehicle, his swagger giving off a very George Clooney vibe. When he came inside, everyone turned to him.

"Everything okay in here?" he asked, glancing around the room from one suspect to the next.

"They were just leaving," I said.

No one moved.

"Well?" Jordan said loudly. "You heard the lady. Everyone out unless you're going to buy something."

As they filed toward the door, Catherine shot me a glare, and so did Doctor Butte. Charlie cradled Doreen, and for a moment, I was envious of their relationship. Of their closeness. They cared so deeply for each other and I wondered if I'd ever have that in my life.

"Are you okay?" Jordan asked once the door had closed.

I pushed my glasses up my nose and nodded. Still furious that he'd put me at the top of Sheriff Richards' suspect list, I remained quiet.

He chuckled and shook his head. "I can see by the way you're glaring at me that you're angry I did my job. I had to tell her about the letter."

"What letter?" Annabelle asked.

"The letter Bonnie's lawyer gave to me stating that I would inherit the store," I replied. "That's what the sheriff was after the day she came in."

She furrowed her brow. "Wait a minute. You knew before today that the store was yours?"

I nodded.

"Why in the world didn't you tell me?" she shrieked. "I've been worrying myself to death over here, wondering if I'm going to have a job or not!"

"I… I wasn't sure," I muttered.

"You weren't sure you wanted the store, or you weren't sure you were going to keep me on?" she asked. "Sam, I need this job!"

"No. I wanted you here, I just… I wasn't sure if you were the killer. I thought that maybe you killed Bonnie hoping that the store would be left to you."

She stared at me a long moment with her mouth agape. "Sam!"

"I'm sorry, Annabelle. You were with her that morning. Sage Advice is so important to you… I couldn't rule you out as a suspect."

"Wait a minute," Jordan said, holding out his hand. "Annabelle was with Bonnie the morning she was killed?"

We both ignored him.

Placing her hands on her hips, Annabelle pursed her lips. "I'm so totally offended right now. How could you think I was a killer?"

I shrugged and searched the air for the right words. "Evidence pointed to it. I… I had to be sure, Annabelle."

"And now?"

"I know it wasn't you."

"And what changed your mind?" she asked.

I sighed, hating my next words. "Because I just realized who killed Bonnie."

"Who?" Jordan asked. "Who murdered Bonnie?"

CHAPTER 18

BEFORE I SAID ANYTHING MORE, I had to be sure. Having been thrown under the bus in my past life for a crime I didn't commit and losing everything, I wouldn't do that to someone else. Especially someone I liked.

"Stay here," I said, self-loathing seething from me for what I was about to do. "I'll phone you in a bit."

Once again, I borrowed Annabelle's car and made the now familiar drive to the Tupper farm. My stomach flipped as I pulled up behind Charlie's pickup truck parked in front of the house.

With a long sigh, I exited the vehicle and hurried up the stairs to the front door. Glancing around, I wished I could appreciate the beauty of the farm, but instead, I fought the desire to vomit. As I knocked on the screen door, I almost hoped no one was home. A bird chirped somewhere in the distance, a light breeze running through the cornfield, making the stalks sway. The fall sun provided a bit a warmth, even with the slight chill in the air. Dwarf cows and baby goats spoke to each other in the barn while Daisy barked from inside. A perfect day on the farm, until now. When the door opened, I came face to face with Doreen. She'd taken off the bright scarfs she usually wore on her head, and for the first time, I could see just how sick she was. She seemed to have aged significantly from when she was in the store just a while ago.

"Sam! Come in." She pushed on the screen. "What a lovely surprise!"

I overcame the urge to run, stepped inside and followed her into the living room where I sank down into the cracked brown couch. Daisy wagged her tail and licked my hands as I stroked her pretty blonde head.

"Can I get you something?" she asked. "Lemonade? A soda?"

My stomach rolled. *Pepto Bismol would be*

better. "No, thank you," I said. "I'm fine. Is Charlie home?"

She nodded and took a seat across from me. "Charlie!" she yelled. "We've got company!"

Heavy footsteps sounded from down the hall. "Hey, Sam!" he said as he entered, then sat next to Doreen. "To what do we owe this surprise?"

"I wanted to talk to you about Bonnie," I said, clenching my hands into fists in my lap as I glanced at Catherine's picture, hating the woman even more than I had the previous day. If I was right, she was partially responsible for Bonnie's death.

"What's up?"

Both stared at me expectantly and I tried to recall if I'd ever had a more uncomfortable conversation. The answer was a flat, assured nope. "Well, I've been thinking about the reading of the will."

"Go on," Charlie urged. "You seem quite troubled."

That's putting it mildly. I glanced over at Catherine's picture once again, hoping I was correct in my analysis. If not, there was going to be a lot of hurt feelings. "Everyone there had no idea if Bonnie had left them something or not. I mean,

I'm assuming they guessed she had, but they didn't know for certain."

"That's true," Charlie said, nodding. "The instructions were clear: everyone needed to be at the memorial and the reading of the will to receive their inheritance."

"Awful morning," Doreen muttered, shaking her head. "Just awful."

"Everyone there had no idea what they would be receiving… except you," I continued. "Bonnie's lawyer mentioned that she had planned to tell you about the thirty thousand dollars she'd left. And she did."

"Yes, you're correct. A week or so before she died," Charlie continued. "She wanted us to know she was putting her affairs in order because of her health issues."

Wait a minute. I didn't know Bonnie had anything wrong with her. "What health issues?" I asked, now doubting myself and my theory of who had killed her.

"She had recently been diagnosed with an untreatable brain tumor," Doreen said. "The three of us had always been close while raising Catherine, so she confided in us. We actually joked about being cancer sisters, although it wasn't very funny. Cancer can be a very lonely diagnosis, and it helps to talk to people who are in the trenches with you."

I swallowed past the bile rising in my throat. Had Annabelle known about Bonnie's diagnosis? I glanced at Catherine's photo again. Had Bonnie shared the news with her daughter? Was I wrong about everything? Had Catherine killed her mother?

"What does any of this have to do with the reading of the will?" Charlie asked.

"Did Bonnie ever share with you that she wasn't going to leave anything to Catherine?" I asked.

Charlie shook his head. "When we discussed it, she hadn't made up her mind. I, for one, wish she hadn't left things on such a sour note, but what's done is done."

Feeling a little better, I took a deep breath. "Bonnie brought you all together for the reading for a reason," I said. "Spite would be my guess. She wanted Doctor Butte there so she could insult him one last time. She wanted Catherine there to receive nothing so she'd know her mother died still holding anger within her heart. And, finally, she wanted you there to receive thirty thousand dollars to rub it in Catherine's face."

"That sounds like Bonnie," Charlie said. "It's definitely not a godly way of life, but I agree with all that. Bonnie did have a mean streak."

Doreen nodded. "She was a bit passive aggressive. Always had been."

"You were the only ones who knew exactly what was going to happen at that meeting," I continued. "And you both benefitted from Bonnie's death."

It's been in my family for a few generations. Costs a pretty penny to run it, though.

"I don't think I like what you're saying, Sam," Charlie said. "Are you insinuating that we killed Bonnie to benefit ourselves?"

"Yes." I sighed and closed my eyes for a moment. "You told me this farm is very expensive to run and has been in your family for a long time. You'd want to preserve it for your son and future generations, and thirty thousand dollars would definitely help you achieve that goal."

Charlie stared at me for a long time, then burst out laughing. "Is this some type of joke?" He glanced from me to Doreen, whose features had settled into seriousness, not a hint of a smile to be found. Charlie shook his head. "Are you both trying to pull my leg? That was a good one. I thought for a second you were serious."

I met Doreen's gaze and noted the truth there. She found nothing funny about the situation. In fact, tears welled in her eyes. At that moment, I knew I'd been right. She'd killed Bonnie.

Perhaps I should be relieved that I had solved the crime, but instead, sorrow settled around me like a heavy, wet blanket. "Doreen?" I said softly, fighting back my own sobs. "Do you want to tell me what happened?"

As she stared at her hands, tears fell onto them.

"What are you talking about?" Charlie snapped, now angry. "Doreen didn't have anything to do with Bonnie being murdered!"

She placed her hand on his. "Sam's right, Charlie," she said quietly. "I did kill Bonnie."

I sighed in relief, but my heart also twisted with pain. No longer was I on the suspect list, and neither was anyone else. Yet, Bonnie, who was terminal, was about to spend the rest of her years in a courtroom, and possibly prison, if she lived that long.

"How did you figure it out?" she asked. "I thought we were home scot-free."

The fact she was willing to let someone else take

the fall for her deed irritated me to no end. I could've gone to prison, as well as her stepdaughter, Catherine. Even if there was no love lost between the two, I found it upsetting that she been willing to have Catherine convicted. And then there was Annabelle… she wouldn't last a day in prison.

I took a deep breath and put my thoughts in order. "First, Bonnie's lawyer shared with me that you were getting some money from her. I asked if she had told you about it, and he said that she had discussed it, but he didn't know if she'd shared the news with you. I guessed that Bonnie had told you about it, and it turns out I was right."

Poor Charlie's face paled as he grabbed his wife's hand.

"Second, you've got cancer," I continued. "I can't imagine the medical bills. Between those and the farm, you desperately need Bonnie's money." Not mentioning that I'd spied on them at the church seemed like a good idea. Catherine had stolen from them, which only added to their financial burden.

"We don't need the money bad enough for Doreen to commit murder!" Charlie yelled.

"She already admitted to it," I replied softly. "I'm sorry, Charlie."

He turned to her and grabbed Bonnie's shoulders. "Is this true? You did this?"

"I did," she said, lifting her chin defiantly. "We are heavily in debt, and Bonnie's money will help immensely. All I want is for you to be able to keep the farm after I'm gone, to give it to our kids and grandkids, Charlie. I want to keep it in our family."

Shaking his head, he shut his eyes and dropped his hands to his lap. "What have you done?" he whispered.

"Why didn't you just wait for Bonnie to pass?" I asked. "Why kill her when she had the incurable brain tumor?"

"Because we've got a note coming due on the farm and we don't have the money to pay it," Doreen replied. "All my doctor bills have sucked away what little savings we have, thanks to Catherine. And for what? I'm dying anyway. We should have saved the money on my so-called treatment and kept up with the bills. If we default on the note, we lose the farm. I wasn't going to allow that to happen."

"Doreen, you're out of your mind!" Charlie said. "We had to get you treatment! There was a chance that you'd be okay!"

"I'd rather be dead than see my family in the financial trouble we're in," Doreen shot back.

Charlie set his elbows on his knees and cradled his head in his hands, his shoulders shaking as if he was crying.

"How did you do it?" I asked. "How did you end up on the Riverwalk with Bonnie that morning?"

Doreen sighed and rubbed her temples with her forefingers. "At first, I was going to do it in her apartment, but just as I got there, she was leaving. I followed her and hoped for an opportunity. She met with Annabelle. They had coffee and then headed for the Riverwalk. I almost turned back then because I didn't think I'd be able to carry out my plan, but something told me to keep going. When Annabelle suddenly left, I saw my chance.

"I followed her until we reached the secluded area of the Riverwalk. I acted like it was a surprise to see her and gave her a hug. That's when... when I stabbed her." She stared at the wall as she told her tale, as if she could see the scene play out there. "I pushed her in the water and when she was dead... I walked away."

"What have you done?" Charlie whispered.

"Why, Doreen? We would've been okay. You didn't need to do this."

As my eyes welled, I pulled out the phone from my pocket. I stood and stepped outside, shutting the screen door behind me, wishing I felt better about catching the killer. I could only hope the police and courts had mercy on her.

With shaky hands, I dialed Jordan as I sat down on the stairs.

"Where are you?" he asked, picking up after the first ring.

"I'm at the Tupper farm," I said, shutting my eyes against the sun, wishing the breeze could carry away the heaviness in my heart. "Doreen did it. She killed Bonnie."

Silence stretched between us as I concentrated on the sun warming my face.

"How did you get her to confess?" he asked.

"I just asked her, Jordan. I guess I asked the right questions at the right time."

"You better get out of there," he replied. "She may try to kill you so she doesn't pay for what she's done."

I glanced over my shoulder and found Doreen and Charlie in an embrace, both sobbing uncontrollably. "I don't think I have to worry about that. I'll wait here for you."

"On my way." In the background, I heard his car door shut and the ignition fire up.

"Jordan?"

"Yes?"

"Don't come in here with sirens and guns blazing," I said. "It's not necessary. Please be gentle with her."

CHAPTER 19

I ARRIVED BACK at the store right before closing time to find Aiden, the developers' representative, waiting for me.

"We'd like to make you an offer," he said, flashing me his best smile. In the daylight, his demeanor reminded me a bit of Gilbert Gottfried.

"It's not for sale," I said.

He wrote down a number and slid it across the counter to me. I didn't bother to look, and slid it right back.

"Everyone has a price," he said, jotting down another number.

"I don't," I replied. "I've made a promise to keep this building and this store. I can't sell it to you even if I wanted to, which I don't."

"Sure you can!" he exclaimed. "We can help you get around all the legal paperwork and—"

"Listen to me, Aiden. It's not going to happen. Not today, not tomorrow. And frankly, I suggest you look for somewhere else to build your hotel. Heywood doesn't want you. We like it just the way it is. We don't want your development."

"It's a boon for the economy."

He liked to say that. I sighed and shut my eyes for a moment, completely exhausted. "I'm going to tell you this one time, then I'm calling the cops. Get. Out. Of. My. Store."

With a huff, he pivoted on his loafer and exited.

Although I'd have preferred not to talk to anyone for the rest of the day, I turned to Annabelle and motioned her into the back room. We had to have an important conversation.

As I plopped down on the stool at the back workstation, she finished up the last transaction. A moment later, the front door clicked, signaling it had been locked, and she hurried into the back room and sat on the stool next to me.

"Who was that guy?"

"A developer who wants to buy the store, Knit Wit, and some other properties so he can build a hotel here."

"Oh. We don't want a hotel."

"That's what I told him."

"So, you aren't selling?"

I shook my head. "He'll have to step over my cold corpse to get to this store."

"How dramatic," she said, giggling. "On another note, did you find out who killed Bonnie?"

"It was Doreen Tupper."

"Oh, my goodness," she whispered, her mouth forming a perfect O. "What a surprise that is. Why did she do it? How did you figure it out?"

I explained all the details, the pain of it all still twisting my heart.

"Wow. I never would've guessed that, Sam. You're super smart. Are you going to, like, have your name in the papers and stuff?"

That was the last thing I wanted. "No. I told Jordan to keep me out of it. If I never see Barry from the *Sentinel* again, I'll be a happy woman."

Annabelle grinned and arched an eyebrow. "Jordan? Shouldn't that be Deputy Branson to you? Is there a little something brewing between the two of you?"

She snickered as I rolled my eyes. "Of course not. I'm in no shape to even think about dating."

"He's cute in a George Clooney sort of way," she mused. "You'd make a great looking couple."

"Stop," I said, laughing that we both thought he resembled the same celebrity. "It's never going to happen."

"Why not?"

"Because… because I don't want to be involved with any man," I replied, throwing my hands up into the air.

"You don't have to marry him."

"I don't even want to date," I said, shaking my head. "I lost my husband not too long ago."

"Yeah, the guy who blew up your life. I understand. I bet you'll eventually change your mind."

"Nope. With everything going on with the store and me going through menopause, I have no interest in men, nor do I have the patience."

Annabelle rolled her eyes. "You know, I can make you something to help with the menopause, and it may help with the patience issue as well."

Why hadn't it occurred to me that I did now own an herbal store and I was sitting across from a talented herbalist? "I feel dumb for not thinking of that sooner."

"You should feel very stupid," she said, winking. "But let's blame it on the menopause. It's no fun."

"No, it's not," I sighed.

We sat in silence for a moment, then she said,

"But I must know… Did you really think I could murder Bonnie?"

With the laughter we shared, my mood had improved slightly, but now the conversation had taken a serious turn and my smile faded. I nodded.

"I find that fascinating. What about me gave you that idea? Do I like, give off some murderous vibes at times? I don't have them often, but I always thought I hid them pretty well."

I studied her for a long moment then sighed. "Nothing," I said. Annabelle was too innocent, too good of a person to murder anyone, and deep down, I knew that. I realized the only reason I had suspected her was because of my own insecurities and trust issues. "It was my fault, Annabelle. After what happened to me in Hollywood, I find it very difficult to believe in people. My husband… I'm not sure I ever really knew him. And my so-called friends… everyone abandoned me when I needed them most. I haven't gotten over any of it."

She pursed her lips and nodded. "I get it and I'm sorry that happened to you. If I'd gone through what you did, I'd have trouble trusting people as well."

"I'm so sorry, Annabelle," I whispered, tears

welling in my eyes for the millionth time that day. I hadn't honestly cried this much in years, even when Gerald had been killed. For the cameras— well, that was a different story.

"Hey, I forgive you." She grabbed my hands. "You went through something very traumatic, Sam. When that happens, we can all be a little out of our minds."

"Thanks," I said. "I couldn't believe Bonnie left me the store. I just felt so much pressure. Between that and her murder, I didn't know who I could count on."

"Hey, we're friends now, okay?" she said, smiling. "We're, like, totally fine, Sam."

I glanced around the store. "I meant what I said earlier. I want you to stay here and help me with Sage Advice. I can't do it without you."

Her grin widened as she squeezed my fingers. "I have so many ideas."

"Me, too."

"We're going to make a great team!" she squealed.

Her enthusiasm was contagious. So much so, I almost squealed myself. "Agreed."

"Do you think we should open the tea shop first, or get an online store going?" I asked.

Annabelle tapped her forefinger against her

lips. "I was going to say the tea shop, but winter is almost here and it'll be too cold to sit outside. Maybe we should, like, look into seeing what's involved in an online store?"

"I can talk to Colin Breckshire about it," I said. "That was Bonnie's lawyer, and he's agreed to be mine."

"Oh, that's great news. I've been doing some studying on online marketing," Annabelle said. "For Facebook and Instagram. Once I have those down, we can talk about TikTok."

I grimaced at the mention of social media.

"What's wrong?"

"I hate all that," I said. "I used to be forced to post things on Instagram. I just felt like it's a violation of my privacy."

"So I guess you don't want to be the online face of Sage Advice then?"

"No! Absolutely not!" Even though my physical appearance had changed quite a bit, I feared I'd still be recognized by my former colleagues. And the paparazzi... if they discovered me, they'd descend onto Heywood and end my private life, causing more drama than even Cassie would want.

"Okay, we'll figure something out. In the meantime, I'm off. I've got a hot date."

"Really? Who is it?" I barely knew the woman before me at all. Yes, we'd worked together, but I'd been so worried about my true identity being revealed, I hadn't made any attempts to get to know her. Since I hadn't seen her with a man, I'd assumed she wasn't dating anyone.

Annabelle snorted, rolled her eyes and stood. "It's me, a glass of wine, and the movie, *The Breakfast Club*. It'll be my fiftieth time watching it."

I could barely watch reruns of my favorite shows, let alone the same movie fifty times. "Do you know the script?"

"Most of it," she replied. "It's a classic, though."

I'd seen it maybe two or three times when it first came out ages ago, but I hadn't watched it recently and really didn't remember most of it. I did recall I had a crush on the bad boy played by Judd Nelson.

"At some point, I'd like to hear stories from your life as Samantha Rathbone," Annabelle continued. "If you're willing to share."

The long work days, fighting with the director of *As the Years Turn*, Davey, over my aging and weight, and attending dinners and fundraisers… it all seemed so empty now. My current situation was much more fulfilling to me. But that didn't mean I didn't have a few good stories. "I can tell you about the time I met Simon Le Bon from Duran Duran at a party in Beverly Hills," I teased, knowing she'd want to stick around for it.

"Oh, my gosh. You're so lucky," Annabelle said, sitting on the stool once more. "Please. Tell me everything!"

~

THAT NIGHT, I sat on my sofa and studied an herbalism book, reading up on Black Cohosh and its effects on menopause. It sounded quite promising. As another hot flash hit and my insides felt like they were melting, I decided to talk to Annabelle about the herb in the morning and see if she'd recommend a tincture or capsule. Or maybe she had some other suggestions, something I hadn't yet run across in my research.

I shut the book and leaned my head back against the cushions, waiting for my body to cool down. Catnip sat at my side, purring. As I stroked him, I was surprised by how much he calmed me, how much I enjoyed having him around. Why in the world had I never had pets before this? "Things are changing in a good way, right, Catnip?"

He glanced up at me from under hooded lids.

"You and me, buddy. We're starting over and our lives are going to be great. Big, bold plans are in the works."

Goosebumps spread over my skin as I thought of the future. Getting the online store up and running I assumed would be challenging, but in the end, I hoped it would be worth it. Once the winter snow cleared, we could set some tables out in front of the store to serve tea. Maybe, just maybe, there would be a way to build some sort of decking out the back looking over the river to expand the teashop. Expensive, yes, but somewhere in the future, it may be a great source of income. All the restaurants, the ice cream store, and even Knit Wit had a patio or deck. Sage Advice was the only building besides the church that didn't. Annabelle had told me, during the spring and summer, the knitting club met outside where they drank wine and talked about their projects as they worked their needles. Sage Advice needed to step up its game. I only wished I had the money to start it now, and I considered petitioning for my paychecks that were tied up in the bank accounts the Feds had seized to pay for retribution for Gerald's embezzlement. But that would mean the police would be aware I ended up in Heywood and my anonymity would be destroyed.

Catnip jumped from the couch and stalked over to the door. Ugh. Not again.

I dropped to the floor and crawled over next to him, making a mental note to have the carpet cleaned. He stared at the crack underneath the door, his tail swishing once again.

Leaning my head against the panel, I closed my eyes and listened. The old building moaned and groaned as it settled in for the night. Was Catnip focused on that? Or was there something else out there?

He meowed loudly and I placed my finger over my lips as if he should know that meant to be quiet. Silly of me. Was that scratching I heard?

Catherine had already admitted she'd been sneaking around in Bonnie's place. Did she return? If so, how? By busting in through the back door again? My fury surged. She had no business being in my building.

I stood and hurried over to the kitchen where I grabbed my mace from on top of the refrigerator. Creeping back over to the door, my heart thundered as I gripped the canister. Did I have the safety off? I twisted the top, just to be certain.

Hopefully, if I needed to use the weapon, I wouldn't spray myself.

Placing my hand on the doorknob, I took a few deep breaths, then flung it open and jumped into the hallway. The light from my apartment illuminated the space, and I screamed at my discovery, causing Catnip to escape into the bedroom with a loud hiss.

A mouse. A furry brown mouse with big brown eyes stared up at me, then scampered away.

I had a mouse in my building. Would coming face to face with a murderer be better or worse?

Hurrying back into my apartment, I slammed the door and leaned against it, dropping the mace canister to the carpet.

Moments later, Catnip stalked back into the room and glared at me with his wide green gaze.

"I'm sorry. You're right. It was a complete overreaction."

I then realized that I had the solution to my mouse problem staring at me with a critical eye. I'd been debating whether to let my new friend loose to run the building, and the decision had just been made for me. He hardly ever slept at night, anyway.

I opened the door and pointed into the hallway. "Go and kill that thing and any of its friends."

He didn't move.

"Please?"

He glanced from me to the hallway and back.

"I'd really appreciate it."

Nothing.

"I'll give you some milk."

With that, he stalked out into the hallway. I swore he understood everything I said to him and just ignored me most of the time.

EPILOGUE

Two months had passed since I'd become owner of Sage Advice. I'd poured my heart and soul into the store, working sometimes as many as sixteen hours a day. Annabelle had been by my side for most of it. She'd dubbed us the Superior Sisters. Most of the time, I felt we lived up to the name. Sometimes, I preferred the Disappointing Duo, especially when it came to the business side of running the store. I'd substituted my herbal books for entrepreneurial tomes and studied nightly, while also spending far more time on the phone with Colin Breckshire III than I wanted to.

Setting up the online store proved more difficult than either Annabelle or I imagined, especially since neither of us were particularly computer literate. In my past life, my computer time had consisted of checking my email and posting to social media. Building an online store was out of my wheelhouse.

Annabelle had the brilliant idea of hiring a high school kid to do it. We figured it would take him a week or so and budgeted to pay him. In reality, he completed the set up in just under two hours and did a beautiful job. Even the photos he took of the products we wanted to list looked as if they'd been done by a professional. I was so impressed I paid him for the week.

I'd also been spending what free time I had with Gina from File It Away. Annabelle joined us for coffee or cocktails and even adopted one of Gina's rescue dogs, a seven-year-old Beagle named Ralphie who liked to take a walk in the morning and sleep all day. Annabelle said it was like he was meant to be hers because he fit into her life so perfectly. Even Catnip liked him, and the two napped at the store together most of the day. When we closed for lunch, Annabelle and I took both for a walk. Catnip hated the leash but didn't mind me carrying him.

One day, as Annabelle and I were strolling

along the Riverwalk, my phone rang. Normally, I'd ignore it, but glancing at my screen, I realized it was Gina.

"Hey," I answered. "What's up?"

"I need your help," she whispered.

Grabbing Annabelle's arm, we came to a halt. "What's going on, Gina?"

Annabelle's brow furrowed in concern.

"It's my ex-husband," she whispered. "He's dead."

"Ralph's dead?" I asked. Annabelle gasped and placed her head next to mine so she could hear. How weird was it that both of my friends had dated and/or married the same man?

"Yep. Dead as dead can be, and the police think I did it, Sam. I'm in big trouble. I need your help."

Annabelle and I exchanged glances. "Where are you?" I asked.

"At File It Away. The police are in the front room. I said I had to use the bathroom and I called you."

"We have to help her," Annabelle whispered. I nodded in agreement.

"We're on our way, Gina."

I wasn't sure exactly what we could do to help

her, but I knew in my heart she didn't kill Ralph... no matter how much he deserved it.

NEXT UP IN the Heywood Herbalist Cozy Mysteries: Lavender and Lies. Grab your copy today!

ABOUT THE AUTHOR

Carly Winter is the pen name for a USA Today best-selling and award-winning romance author.

When not writing, she enjoys spending time with her family, reading and enjoying the fantastic Arizona weather (except summer - she doesn't like summer). She does like dogs, wine and chocolate and wishes Christmas happened twice a year.

For more information on her books, please visit:
CarlyWinterCozyMysteries.com